HOOKED
MERCILESS FEW MC

S. COURTNEY

CHAPTER ONE

HOOKED
THE MERCILESS FEW MC: DEVIL'S IGNITED
Haverhill, VT

Jett, aka Fiend

I deserve to die for what I've done to my brothers.

Instead of seeking help from them, I chose to self-medicate, hoping each hit would keep me in a drug-induced haze to drown out the pain from the past and the stress of keeping up the charade that I'm okay.

Now, I'm pressing against the gaping wound in my stomach to avoid bleeding out faster.

Even after all my secrets and indiscretions, the betrayal... my brothers tell me to hold on...

I don't deserve to. I don't deserve them.

"It's okay," Offering them a forced smile. I coughed and saw the blood in the palm of my hand. "You don't need me."

Ultimately, I made the decision to let go...

Before joining the Merciless Few: Devil's Ignited chapter of Massachusetts, I was Jett Watkins from Haverhill, Vermont.

I suffered from a classic case of middle child syndrome. Nestled between my sisters, who thrived on torturing and teasing me like siblings do. I was the golden child, the first boy, until eight years later when my twin brother and sister were born, and then I was another mouth to feed. I missed that spotlight focus on me, and I found that acting out was a way to get close to that. It started with a failed test here and there, Mom would lecture me while Dad stood as the authority figure, classic good cop/bad cop scenario. It went in one ear and out the other while simultaneously giving me that dopamine hit of attention. I leveled up to ditching a class I hated anyway or the entire day, and my friends only encouraged it. In one of his usual outbursts he said I was hanging out with a 'bad crowd.'

My sisters thought I was a brat, acting out because Kat and Dog were born. That's their nickname, but Katarina and Douglas weren't a burden; they looked up to me. I should have been a shining example for them, but when I saw them get endless attention, I felt the urge to misbehave.

I guess when I was caught underage drunk driving and wrapping the car around a tree, was when I first felt genuine disappointment from everyone.

The worst part of it all was that no one ever said anything to my face; I heard it while I was unconscious.

The door creaked, which brought me into some state of awareness.

I felt a hand brush my hair away. I was going through an emo phase, brushing my dark hair forward to cover my face before I started growing it out. Then I felt a soft kiss, and I knew it was Mom. "Be careful when you hold his hand. Watch the tubes."

"Mama, is Rocket going to die?" I heard Kat's voice crack.

"No, your brother is resting so his body can heal. It'll only be for a few more days, and then you can tell him how much you missed him, okay?"

"Okay. I love you, Rocket. I can't wait for you to get better. We can have a big tea party!" She was barely a teenager and always held this childlike innocence and curiosity. I felt her let go, and then another hand squeezed mine.

"My sweet baby, I know you can hear me. Why would you do this to yourself? This isn't my chipmunk. Your father is still upset, but I promise I'll get him to come."

Apparently, you can still get angry even while unconscious. Of course, he wasn't here. Work always took top priority over everything. My dad tried to force his beliefs on me, and when I outright refused, he set his sights on Dog. When Dog

showed his compliance, suddenly, I was the big letdown, the black sheep. Because I didn't want to toil in the mill and wither away, slaving until I died. I knew he said yes out of intimidation and fear. I won't let him end up a puppet. And I would carve my own path.

I don't know how much time had passed, but eventually, I opened my eyes. The starkness of the hospital lights made my eyes water. The lady, who I assume is my nurse, was happy to see me looking back when she came in for her routine check-in.

"Mr. Watkins, it's good to see you awake. Let me raise your bed. You'll be more comfortable."

I groaned, feeling this burning, sharp pain. "A...a mirror," I remember feeling that moment when the hot metal slammed against my neck and collarbone. The force caused me to black out in pain until now.

There was a scar there; it would be a permanent reminder in addition to the memories and the inevitable rant my father would go on.

She goes and comes back in with a hand mirror. I immediately looked at my face, which was bruised and swollen. I was lucky my eyes weren't blacked from the airbag deploying, but I did have a busted lip. My hands were shaky as I moved the view lower and saw what I felt: a tight bandage around my neck and shoulder. I used my dominant hand, but somehow, I felt this tingly sensation where the

bandage was, and I dropped the mirror into my lap, unable to hold it up any longer.

"How long do I have to keep this bandage on?"

"It depends on what the doctor says, and how fast you heal, Sug. Don't you worry about that. Thank God you opened your eyes again and got a second chance!" She said happily.

"Yeah, a second chance to wind up in jail. They'll arrest me the moment I'm well enough." I look away to avoid the tears and keep my throat from tightening up.

She sat on my bed and took my hand. "Listen, you made some mistakes, but the good Lord saw fit to give you a second chance to make them right. Now, you'll have to face whether you serve time or not, but you have a long life ahead of you, and some lessons have to be learned. Don't get too caught up in the first one."

I like how she assumed I was squeaky clean until this incident. I sigh and groan as a sharp pain shoots up the middle of my back. I hissed as I tried to lay on my side, but it was worse. She observed me, "It's time for your dose. Let me grab the cart."

I take the remote and turn on the TV. I was afforded the

luxury of hospital TV and the vast selection of 13 channels, so I put it on a game show when she returned with a needle in hand—a huge needle.

She's close enough to read her name tag, Sadie. She takes the alcohol pad, and I hold my arm out, but she shakes her head. "Shift over. It's going in your back."

"What, no way!"

"Do you want the pain to go away quicker? It needs to go near the epicenter, and it looks like it's your back. Now, am I wrong?" She wasn't, but the size of the needle compared to her hand made me question whether I should tough it out. She waves her hand in front of me to get my attention, "If I shoot you in the arm, it's going to take 20 minutes. Can you handle another 20 like this?"

Another lightning bolt of pain, "Ahhhh! No!" I screamed and shifted over. A needle in the back had to be way better than this excruciating pain and pulsing.

She rubbed the pad between my shoulder blades, and I second-guessed my decision.

"Take a deep breath and count to five out loud."

I inhale deeply, then count, "Five...four...three...ahh fuck goddammit! ARGH!"

I knew she would do it early, but I didn't expect the burning sensation to trigger more pulsing! I bit my pillow to keep from releasing a string of curses that would make the Devil blush.

"Okay, okay. Breathe and lean back. It should subside in five minutes or less. In the meantime, I'll grab your dinner and an extra dessert!"

She looked back at me and smiled, "Count your blessings, Mr. Watkins. You're here for a reason."

I had no idea what that reason was.

CHAPTER TWO

HOOKED
THE MERCILESS FEW MC: DEVIL'S IGNITED
Haverhill, VT

The next few days went well. Mom visited daily and apologized every time for my father's absence. At this point, I didn't want to see him or hear his rant about how this affects everyone, instead of wondering why I did what I did.

Then it all went to shit. The sheriff's office came into my room and stated I have a trial date 45 days from now. I was going to be charged with DWI, but since I am just shy of 18, the most I could get was 12 months. I would spend it in juvie until I turned 18, and then they would transfer me to jail to finish the rest of my time. I also had an $8000 fine, community service, and my license would be suspended. They would consider good behavior based on my school performance and character witnesses.

I was screwed. My guidance counselor said if I didn't get my act together, I wouldn't graduate. I didn't want that; I was having fun. I know my teachers wouldn't vouch for me and my family...well, mom would portray the heartbroken mother who wants better for her child if they gave me a second chance. My dad would recommend a harsher sentence or boot camp to make me someone else's problem.

The sound of my door opening rattles me, and there's my dad, still in his soot-covered coveralls; at least his face and hands were clean. He steps in to let the door close behind him but doesn't come closer.

It's awkward silence until I break it. "Did you come here to stare at your failure of a son, or did you come to say something? Oh, and if it's your usual bullshit capped off with had you listened to me, you'd be in one piece spiel, then save it, Dad."

He looked stunned. What's funny is that it was like I was yelling at myself. I was a spitting image of him with wavy dark brown hair and matching eyes—nothing special, but I also inherited his sharp jawline and bad temper.

His stunned look was replaced by his usual stoic one. "It's good to see you awake, son."

Is it?

I noticed his word choice of good to see you instead of glad to see you—the least emotion-filled response.

"Thank you."

"You're lucky I have such an outstanding report within the community and with Sheriff Tate. They're willing to lessen the charges if you agree to work in the mill to become an upstanding Haverhill citizen like me. It could even count toward your community service."

I felt my jaw tighten as I shook my head. "Grandpa said you would do this, but he said the cycle should stop with me, and on his grave, I'm going to see that it does! I'm in control of my own life decisions!"

"And look where it got you! You're a goddamn criminal! My son is a criminal! By the way, my father was a stubborn old fool. He instilled these values in me, so why wouldn't I do the same with my sons?"

"Because it took you away from us! There was no family; it was a mom raising five kids alone while you worked these long hours. Mom was the perfect wife, but she couldn't deal with this alone! She looked for you and found a temporary fix! Do you even care that she tries to put on the perfect wife role while strung out to escape the pressure?" He seemed shocked to know that mom was using drugs to cope; how else was she supposed to manage?

I scoffed at his sad attempt to feel pity, "You know, at one point, I thought maybe you were having an affair. It would have made more sense, but you work to get away. You'd rather be there than with us."

"You're right! I'd rather be there or at the bar than deal with a disobedient son who would waste his opportunity to become a proper man!"

"A man?! A man cares for his family, loves them, shows affection, and only wants the best for them. You want me and Dog to become you, and I'll be damned if I do..."

"Then I want you out of my house!"

"Fine! I'm surprised you even know where that is!"

His ears were red hot, and I'm sure mine were too. I couldn't wait to get away. I already had parts of the plan flushed out. My grandfather had given me access to a secret account. I also saved some money from yard work, and mom passed me a twenty from time to time just because. I would take some of that money, buy my first motorcycle, and make my way to Briarswood, Massachusetts, where the closest Merciless Few chapter was located.

The Merciless Few was a biker club hell-bent on saving good souls, tormented, and abused by any means necessary. They lived the life I wanted, kicking my boots up in the breeze and having any girl I wanted. They called them club bunnies, or bunnies for short, and they wouldn't be able to keep their hands off me. I'd have a camaraderie with my brothers that I couldn't get at home. I knew my place was with them. Now, with my dad's ultimatum to get out, I would become a fugitive of the law.

The big question was, how do I say goodbye to my family? Each of the grandchildren received the same share of funds, released on our 16th birthday. I don't think Dog & Kat know about it, so I snuck it into their letters and told them to follow their dreams, not anybody else's. I apologized to my mother for breaking her heart but told her how much she meant to me. Because of her, my heart would never turn cold and emotionless like my father. I told my older sisters to take care of Mom and remind her that this was not her fault and that I made this decision alone. I ended their letter telling them that although we didn't get along, I always loved them and knew they were the ones who kept me grounded.

I stashed the letters until I was released. I took the time to carve my path out, and in no time, I would be a Merciless Few brother.

I hope.

CHAPTER THREE

HOOKED

THE MERCILESS FEW MC: DEVIL'S IGNITED
Haverhill, VT

One week later...

Miss Sadie smiled: "Good morning, my handsome Jett! Aren't you happy to be released today?!" She didn't know how much her cheery disposition kept me going through the excruciating pain, the tests, and the determination of whether I would need physical therapy or not. If she weren't here, I would have given up long ago.

The battle scar and my beat-up mug told how bad the wreck was. I had a hard time dealing with the pulsing pain and soreness; they only got better with medication.

"I sure am. I've got a new life to build."

"That's good to hear. The doctor put in a prescription for your pain meds, which should last for the remaining time it takes that wound to heal properly. After that, any acetaminophen will do. Also, he prescribed an antibacterial cream with anti-itch properties. There is no need to make it worse by all your scratching. See, you're doing it now!" She looked at me and sighed, mussing my hair. "You take care of yourself and live up to those words you told your father. Be your own man, not what he wants you to be."

"You heard that?"

We were screaming at each other by the end of the conversation. I shouldn't be surprised. She smiled. "Mmm hmm, sometimes dads can be wrong. Prove your worth, make yourself proud."

That gave me the confidence in my decision to move on. "I will, Miss Sadie."

They asked if they should call my family a few hours later, and I declined. I took a cab and snuck back into the house. Fortunately, everyone was at church. I packed two bags, placed the letters where they could find them, and left my cell phone, my dad's last chokehold on me. Lastly, I grabbed my wallet to pay the cabbie who would drop me off at a hotel near this motorcycle dealership in the next town. I transferred my funds to my new checking account and removed my parents' permission to access my old account. My dad wouldn't hesitate to freeze it. He still might, even though there's no money in it.

I look back at the slightly off-white farm home with the fluted-shaped wind chimes and rocking chairs and give it a little wave. I know the moment I got settled at home, the cops would come to arrest me, and my father would happily open the door.

The next day, my first day of freedom, I strolled into the authorized Harley Davidson bike shop, and my eyes immediately locked on an all-black Scout Sixty. It was modeled after the original 1920s style. Its fuel injection delivers class-leading horsepower and acceleration with a liquid-cooled, 60 cu-in, 78 HP V-Twin engine. It wasn't a Harley, but one day, I'll be able to buy one; until then, this was a classy yet affordable alternative. Once paid, I strapped on one bag, wore the other like a backpack, and started my almost four-hour drive to Briarswood.

Four hours later...

I pass this enormous boulder near the side of the road after this treacherous curve. I can only wonder what would happen to the opposing traffic if it were to rain and they took the curve wrong. Slamming into a boulder is not on my bucket list.

CHAPTER FOUR

HOOKED

THE MERCILESS FEW MC: DEVIL'S IGNITED

Briarswood, Mass.

Three years later...

"It was a good year for the Devil's Ignited, here here?!"

"Hear, hear!" We raise our glasses toward our President. They start to chug their beers, which, hands down, will become a contest. I set my mug down, "Gotta take a leak." I walk back toward mine and Reaper's part of the house. He got patched in way before me and lucked out with the only other ensuite room. I used the one between our doors, the community bathroom. Lucifer had the main ensuite bedroom because he was President and had a wife, Sam. She reminded me so much of my mom. She tried to convince me to connect with my family. "They don't need me, Sam, and I'm with my family. I was meant to be here." She would concede, but there was still that glint of worry in her eyes.

I slipped into my room. I groaned out the pain that I had been hiding since our ride earlier. I was looking for relief at the bottom of my backpack. I heard the familiar sound of rattling. I noted that I only had a few pills left.

The doctor prescribed a 90-day supply with three refills. It seemed excessive, and I wasn't going to refill it until I realized it helped with both my pain and everyday stress. It put me in an almost euphoric high. Soon, I took them like people take their daily vitamins and quickly blew through the prescriptions. Then I found a local physician and complained about my pain, so convincingly I got another year's worth. Then, my luck ran out, and I was on my own.

I needed to find a supplier of something similar, and that's where I fucked up. When I patched in, we were doing jobs for this sloppy, fat fucker named Frankie, who double-crossed his boss and immediately set up the business his way, and now he's the most powerful drug syndicate in the Northeast. We took on jobs for him because he paid almost double that of these smaller businesses. So we became his go-to security to get his shipments to where they needed to go, from the dock or his warehouses to the border where our chapter brothers or other groups would pick up and continue the job to its final destination.

I learned from one of the bunnies that Frankie had every drug imaginable and sold it out of his strip club.

Of all the things I didn't want to do, it sure wasn't groveling to Frankie. I tried to quit and fight the pain with regular over-the-counters, but the effects didn't last nearly as long, and I missed that blissful peace that took me away from my intrusive thoughts about my family, that I wasn't good enough, and a complete waste of space, and they were better off.

Maybe everybody was...

One night, after Dixie was done blowing me, she reached into her purse and pulled out this little purple container before sitting her bare pussy on my stomach and grinding. Sometime between her arrival at the clubhouse and now, her underwear disappeared from her barely covering denim skirt. I was probably her second conquest of the night. She was known to bedhop, but most bunnies did, maybe not Lila; I've never seen her with anyone. I certainly haven't had the opportunity.

Demon was probably Dixie's first stop, and he was known to collect souvenirs in his so-called dungeon.

If she meant anything to me, I'd strum her like a guitar until she came all over me. Instead, I sat up on my elbows, watching her giggle before she popped the pill in her mouth and closed her eyes. The effect looked almost immediate as her hooded eyes stared at me.

Somehow, I knew she was going to wear me out.

"What was that?" I was curious.

"It's Heaven in a little pill. It heightens all my senses, and everything is more. Even rubbing against you feels amazing. Please, let me ride you."

She continues to grind against me, but now she was moaning like a wildcat. Fuck! She peels off her white ribbed crop top, revealing her perfect tits. By perfect, I mean they fit completely in my hands. Taking another pill, she leans forward; her nipples were pierced and begging to be pulled by my teeth. She smiles, "Open up." I ponder for a second, then stick my tongue out. She places it gently, and I take it back. It tastes wretched, but maybe I should have swallowed it immediately and not let it dissolve. Not a second after choking down the pill, her tongue was down my throat. I wrap my arm around her before flipping and tossing her on the bed. She slipped off that yard of fabric she called a skirt and stared at me as I pulled off my cut and hung it on my chair before ripping everything else off. I don't know if it was the rushing hormones or motions to take everything off, but I was hit with an invisible force. It was like hitting a brick wall, but instead of feeling pain, I felt nothing but pleasure. I see Dixie eyeing me, licking her lips. I look down to see my dick stiffer and harder than ever. The tip leaked pre-cum before she even touched me.

"Holy shit..."

"I told you."

I grab her by her ankles and pull her to the edge of the bed. She squeals, "Hurry up while we're both high. It'll be an experience you'll never forget." At that moment, a pulse shot down to my dick, and I quickly slid myself in, groaning in disbelief as she pulsed against me. "Goddammit, Dixie, you're so damn tight...fuck, I'm gonna bust!" I kept the pace slow to avoid it, but she started squeezing in a pattern and bouncing her ass against me. The visual and the feeling had me cumming like a fire hose in under a minute. I grunted as I emptied into her.

Well, that's embarrassing.

But she pulled me down and flipped me, straddling me again, sliding down my still-hardened shaft.

"It's okay. You can blame the pill. I've never had a guy last more than two minutes the first time the first go around, but they completely decimated me in the second round... here's your chance to redeem yourself."

And that's what I did. I fucked her up and down, side to side, and in any other position I could put her in for the next hour. Finally, after my second orgasm and her sixth, she physically tapped and passed out in my bed. I covered her, threw on my boxers, and went out to the bathroom. The enhanced feeling was still raging. I felt amazing as if I could go at least once more. Then, I was interrupted out of my bliss by a knock. More like a bang!

"Stop jerking off in there! A girl's gotta go! Come on!"

I opened the door and pulled in whatever smartass was running her mouth. Poppy looked surprised that we were now in the bathroom together.

"Fiend, I thought you were servicing Dixie?"

Poppy sauntered past me, standing near the toilet. She eyed my rock-hard erection and smirked before pulling her shorts and underwear down to sit. She had no shame at all... and neither did I.

I rubbed my erection and growled as I approached. She looked up through her bangs and licked her lips.

"Suck my dick."

I could hear the night's drinks exiting her system while my dick split her full, pouty lips. She sucked me in as far back as she could without using her hands. She rolled her eyes and exhaled hard. I knew she knew she was tasting Dixie on my cock.

Her continuation said she didn't care as she worked even harder, trying to erase every trace of her off my dick.

My entire body shook as I shot down her throat. Poppy leaned back and swallowed before she grabbed the toilet paper to clean up and wash her hands. I watched her watch me through the mirror.

"Tasty, I'll see you around." She licks the corners of her mouth before exiting the bathroom.

I look at myself in the mirror; this could be a decent substitute. I felt complete and utter euphoria. I went back into my room and passed out.

Sometime later, I felt like I was still sleeping but in a slight state of awareness. I felt this warmth surrounding me, accompanied by this weird sound I couldn't make out, but I could feel my body move in sync. Until I bolt up, growling out my orgasm as Dixie sucks me dry. I flop back down, breathing hard.

She wasn't as mind-blowing as Poppy, but I'd be dead if I said that out loud. I don't play favorites; they're all fair game.

"Good morning. That was my gift to you for last night." She started getting dressed, grabbing one of my T-shirts to cover her. "I might get this back to you." She flashes her pussy again while chuckling.

"No worries. I was wondering, where do you get those pills, and what are they called?"

"They're called cliffhangers. I usually get them at the Dollhouse from the old blonde bartender; you know the one. I flirt. He puts a couple of extras in there for me."

"You ever..." I motion a blow job.

"Fuck no, he's way above my comfort level. Lucifer's the only exception, but Sam would demolish me and bury my body with no remorse. Remember what happened with Reba?!"

She is correct. The rumor has always been that Lucifer is wildly jealous of his baby girl, but Sam is silent and deadly.

I remember that night. Lila and I were chatting at the bar when Reba, one of the long-standing bunnies, stomped in on a mission to take Lucifer from Sam. She drunkenly decreed it the night before, not knowing how loud she was. She also didn't see Sam quietly observing in the kitchen. The darkness behind Sam's eyes freaked me out, but she didn't make a move that night.

The moment Reba stumbled in; I knew chaos was about to

ensue. No matter how many of us told her not to be fucking stupid, including Lucifer himself, she was on a mission to be the Queen Bee.

hiccup "I think it's time for a change in power. We all know I'm the top bitch of this club!"

I guess she was screaming at the top of her lungs to establish dominance, but Lucifer wasn't there, and Sam was in their room. Everyone else was forced to listen to her one-sided tirade.

Lila hopped up quickly. She may be tiny, but she had the balls of a giant.

"Reba, go home before Sam drags your ass up and down this fucking house! You won't win, and he doesn't want you. Have some goddamn respect for yourself!" Lila pushes her toward the door, but she slides around her, "No! This is my clubhouse! I will fight for it!"

Those were her last words as Sam stormed out while cocking her arm back. When she was close enough, she swung, hitting Reba so hard she spun and landed on the floor next to the couch. But she doesn't stay down and charges towards Sam. Demon and I were the only club members there, with Lucifer, Reaper, and Wicked running a small shipment to a local shop. Demon and I were able to separate them, but they tried their best to get at each other by any means necessary.

"Enough!" Lucifer bellowed as he walked into absolute insanity. Sam became very docile. It's rare for him to yell at her, but he was over all this.

"Come here, baby girl." She hesitated before walking into his arms, and she sighed in relief.

"You never have to fight or prove yourself. You're MY #1, no one, and nothing will change that. I married you, Samantha. I love you."

He turned to Reba, "And since you don't seem to understand or respect that, Reba, you're banned from the Merciless Few clubhouse. If you step foot on this property again, I'll let my ol' lady do what she wants."

Reba looked shocked as if she was wronged. We would not witness the reaction to the consequences of her drunken actions when she woke up hungover with a shiner. In her final moments, she screeched at the top of her lungs and then shoved me off her before she walked out. Then the atmosphere cleared, and everybody exhaled before Lila burst out laughing. "I told that stupid bitch to shut the hell up. Now look at her, a whore without a house." Now we're all cracking up.

I walk behind the bar to pour Dixie and I an after fuck shot. The three wise men, equal parts Johnnie Walker, Jack Daniels, and Jim Beam will lessen the effects of being manhandled all night, or it'll put you on your ass. Dixie takes the shot like water and winks at me.

WHOA.

She gathers her things and hops off the barstool, "Hey, I'm going to re-up. Do you want in? One hundred pills for 200 bucks should last you."

I reached into my pocket and handed over the funds, looking around to see who might be around. "Thanks."

"I'll be back later."

And that's how it started. Dixie was my runner for a while, which is good because I hate stepping foot in any of Frankie's establishments. He acted like he owned us when we were doing him a favor while getting paid.

Then life happened, and Dixie fell in love and moved to New Hampshire with her now fiancé, Brutus, a notorious Sinister Skulls member. We live dangerously like any other club, but the Skulls were that 0.1% unhinged, chaotic, territorial bastards. Other clubs move out there way to avoid getting on their shit list. She's in for a wild ride!

I spent the next few weeks trying to wean myself off, but

the shaking and pain seemed to intensify when I tried to. Everything would irritate my scar when brushed against it, and the placement of it made that inevitable. Tank tops, t-shirts, and even my cut caused this mind-numbing sting. Those pills were my relief, dulling the sensation enough to function. I had to lower myself to get my fix.

CHAPTER FIVE

HOOKED
THE MERCILESS FEW MC: DEVIL'S IGNITED
Briarswood, Mass.

I started frequenting the Dollhouse for a quick transaction. After the third or fourth visit, I had to pay the bartender an extra 150 bucks to keep our interactions secret, especially when the group didn't frequent the club due to this long-standing animosity between Frankie and Reaper.

Reaper had a bit of tough luck when he found out his girl was running around on him. What's worse, it caused him to wreck his precious bike. There's nothing worse for a biker than losing the girl who carries him through life with his boots in the breeze.

The accident messed him up good. I had never seen a case of road rash that brutal. Although I was concerned for his physical and, more importantly, mental well-being when we visited the hospital, all I could think about was getting back to the house for another dose. It seemed like any bit of stress, whether mine or someone else's, made me crave a hit.

I could barely handle maneuvering my bike back to the clubhouse. I beelined to my room, paying little attention. I pulled one from my case, "Hey, Fiend, could you..." It was on my tongue when Demon strolled in. I knew it would be suspicious if I blew up at him. I chuckled as I swallowed it, "Since my accident, the doctor put me on pills for...um, pre-diabetes as a precaution. I'm still new to when to take my dose, but I did feel a little dizzy."

His brow raised because, typically, people with diabetes shoot insulin, not take a pill for it. "I can get tattoos with multiple needles, but I can't shoot myself with one, crazy huh?"

"Yeah...anyway, we got a job for Frankie. We'll leave in 30 minutes."

"Okay." Thirty minutes should be enough time for it to hit. The job took little time, a quick run about three towns over. He had a secondary operation there. Backup in case he got shut down here. He may be a sloppy fat fuck, but he was smart. We completed the task for Frankie. What does he want next? To celebrate and host a party at our clubhouse. He has never once 'celebrated' a successful delivery before.

We all knew he was being vindictive since he was now dating, rather, fucking Daisy, Reaper's ex-girlfriend. He couldn't wait to flaunt her around him. My brother was better than me; I'd make sure they'd have to wire his jaw shut and reconstruct an eye socket. But the joke was on Frankie when Daisy secretly ran behind Reap after their confrontation. I know because Daisy bumped into me, almost in tears, on the way out of Reaper's room. I saw Lila in his lap, licking her lips. Lila despised Daisy, and she laid on the sexy-and-willing girl routine thick to stick it to her, but that slut deserved it. Everyone knows she wouldn't be with Frankie if he weren't supplying her.

I may indulge in a pill a time or two, but it doesn't cause me to make stupid decisions. I'm more alert and aware. I perform better in every way. My workouts are longer and more challenging, and my senses are heightened when we're on the open road. Ready to pull the trigger if any highway bandits try to rob us.

I don't have a problem.

Everything was starting to look up, and we even took a night off to party it up at Throttle, our favorite bar. I sit alongside Reaper as we eye our options. "See anything you like?" I asked because I did and was ready to risk it all to feel my dick between new tits.

Then I realize he's not scanning the dance floor. I follow his eyes, and he's watching an interaction between some brunette girl and a drunken idiot. She wasn't interested and made it very clear. The guy gets rough with her, and Reap snaps, almost leaping over the table to put that asshole in a headlock to separate him from the girl. If there's one thing we never tolerate, it's abuse toward women or children. Once he put his hands on her disrespectfully, we knew it was time to mount up because once one of us jumped up, we were all in.

The drunkard saw our crew patch and backed off. The adrenaline made my scar itchy, which brought on the pulsing pain. Now, sitting down was uncomfortable. I walked around before heading to the bar. Mikey, my dealer, strolled up as I rubbed my neck, attempting to focus my attention elsewhere.

"Sup Fiend, it looks like you need some more of your...pain pills, especially if you're going to be participating in more bar fights. I thought you guys were peaceful?"

I glare at him, "I'm fine. Get me a red bourbon shooter." I

didn't want to admit that I was indeed running low and feeling desperate. He knew; it was like he was counting down the number of pills I had and knew when I'd come crawling back. I wouldn't give him the satisfaction with my brothers around. I'd have to sneak back later.

He slides the glass across and then pats his vest pocket. "I'll be here when you're ready."

I found the curvaceous blonde I was leering at earlier, but it turns out she loved pussy as much as I do and wasn't willing to give men another try.

I went home irritated and wanted to feel nothing, to be numb, so I let my intrusive thoughts win. I popped a pill, then had the newly initiated bunny, Kitty, and Poppy servicing my dick simultaneously, using their nails to reach up and trail my chest. It was a tale of old school and new school. Poppy already knew what I liked, but perhaps Kitty could show me something new.

Then they stood up while pushing me on my bed before setting their sights on each other, caressing each other, stripping each other of their clothing. It was quite possibly the hottest thing I ever witnessed.

"So, Fiend...is this what you imagined?" I could tell Kitty was still nervous, following Poppy's lead, but Poppy never took her gaze off me, feeling confident in asking me while making my wildest fantasy come true. This was way more than I expected.

When it came to the girls, it was the brothers' option to break the new bunnies in, sort of a tradition. Most of the time, it was between Demon and me. We would play rock, paper, scissors to see if it was a tag team or one at a time. This time, I lucked out and had my own time with Kitty, and Poppy added herself as a willing bonus. I believe since the bathroom incident, she was trying to lay claim on me, but I wasn't in the market to be tied down; I enjoyed having options.

Wicked was the only brother technically tied down with the twins Tamla and Priya. They were a feisty pair of Indian beauties, and he was afforded a threesome every night. Don't get me wrong—that sounds like a dream—but as the youngest of the group, he seemed already settled down, to a point. He didn't give them the coveted ol' lady status. With two, I'm not even sure he could. That's a unique situation.

Having an ol' lady is not part of my vision as a member of the Merciless Few. Honestly, I don't have a plan for my life; I live it day by day.

Today, I was taking a risk of being seen at the Dollhouse during the day, but there was something wrong with the last dose. It wasn't giving me the feeling of euphoria I was used to. I needed answers.

I slide into the entrance at 3:30 pm, the middle of the day. There's Mikey polishing glasses. I swear he's constantly polishing glasses. He chuckles   before that smug smile crawls across his lips.

"Well, well, well, look who crawled into the viper's den. You know your brother is on Frankie's shit list. What would he think if he knew you were here strung out and begging for another 'prescription'?"

"I'm not strung out. They don't need to know. Now tell me why this batch is trash." I took offense at the name-calling but can't bash my source's face in.

Mickey picks up another glass. "You're going to have to ask Frankie. He's expecting you, anyway." He nodded toward Frankie's office.

Why would he need to see me? Just then, a sharp pain shot across my scar, and my knees almost buckled. At this point, I'd do anything to numb the pain and keep the pulsing from starting. Sometimes, I wonder if the pills cause hallucinations, including this pain. Maybe it was all in my head? The mind itself is a powerful drug, but so is this vice. I know it's real because I had been in pain long before I started taking these pills.

There are days when I want to stop cold turkey, but I can't handle the side effects. Those nights, I hid in my room and slept alone, making sure nobody or bunny saw my night sweats or trying to cover my scar to reduce the irritation, but even skin-to-skin gave me a bolt of pain. However, it's the pulsing pains that almost bring me to my knees, like being sliced open with a blade placed in a fire first.

It's all in your mind, I would tell myself.

Was this punishment for rebelling against my dad? I was a wanted criminal with a father who admitted he'd rather work himself to death than raise his family and love his wife. I never wanted to be anything like him, and being a motorcycle-riding badass was the furthest thing from it.

I knock on his office door. "Come in."

"Oh, for fuck's sake!" I walk in to see Frankie getting a blowjob from Daisy. I am amazed at how low she had sunk from her time with Reaper. She didn't even change the pace of her head bobbing up and down to see who had walked in, and Frankie didn't mind conducting business while she sucked him off.

"Fiend, sit down. You can get next; I'm sure she won't mind." I almost threw up in my mouth. He didn't even look like he was enjoying it.

"I'd rather not. What do you even want, Frankie? Besides doing a job here or there with my brothers, we have nothing to say or discuss, especially now." My eyes lower to her still bobbing. They were short movements which led me to believe that all his cockiness was just that.

Frankie laughs and then takes a bag of pills from his jacket pocket. The amount looks like double my usual order.

"Oh, but we have much to discuss. I know your last batch wasn't up to par, and you're here to re-up, but I have a newer, stronger batch. We gave all you strung-out drug addicts a weak dosage to turn you onto something better."

I didn't like to be grouped in with the drug addicts you see wandering around town doing anything for the next hit, like deep throating someone during a business deal.

"You can have this and more if you keep yourself available to me. Feed me information."

What the hell does that mean? I don't know what information I could provide, but knowing I was purposefully given a placebo to have me come crawling back only pissed me off. "You sneaky son of a bitch! Why would I do you any fucking favors?"

"Because if you don't, I'll make sure your precious club finds out, and you'll never find another sloppy biker group or supplier within the Northeast quadrant. Where will you go, hmm?"

CHAPTER SIX

HOOKED
THE MERCILESS FEW MC: DEVIL'S IGNITED
Briarswood, Mass.

I was at ground zero. My current supply wasn't working, and my mouth was salivating at how much better these could be. Frankie's right, unfortunately. He owned the entire Northeast, and I wasn't strong enough to quit this on my own. I needed my family but couldn't ask for help.

I'd be 'the disappointment' again.

A weak link.

Someone not worth helping, and they'd toss me aside like garbage.

This charade had to continue, but I'd be careful.

"What do you even want?"

"I need a way to get that bastard by himself, to get rid of him. I have plenty of places to hide the body."

I realize she is still down there sucking like a Hoover vacuum. She must be bad at it. Even without the effects of the pills, a bunny usually gets me off in 10 minutes or less. Or maybe Frankie can't stay hard.

She didn't even flinch when he mentioned killing her ex. I know she's not over him that fast. Not the way he was pounding her out; her screams were a testament to that. She never walked the same.

I noticed he was looking at me to help him get Reaper alone. Since he won't give me another pill until there's a solution, I give him one so far-fetched there's no way he'd go through with it.

I shrugged. "Ask him to do a job for you. It's not rocket science."

He stared while tapping his pen. By then, Daisy stood up and slid an aluminum packet from his desk into her bra. She still seemed unfazed about the current conversation and walked out.

This smile formed on his face, "Yeah, seems simple enough. A small shipment from the dock, then I'll put a bullet between his eyes and put him in a shipping container." He laughs.

Although I'm confident it won't work, I still feel guilty for helping.

He tosses the pills, "You're at my beck and call whenever I need you...and I WILL need you as much as you need me. That's all."

I grab the pills and slide them into my pocket.

Hearing those words made me feel like I made a deal with the devil, but after the first test pill, I was willing to play his game. And who says I would have any answers for him anyway? I still control this narrative. Even if he did get the balls to request Reaper, Lucifer would never allow us to go solo. We never go alone. I could tag along, but there's also a risk of

Reaper killing Frankie for everything he put him through, and I lose my pipeline. And if they found out I was involved...

When I return, Reaper and I are tasked with getting groceries for the B.A.C.A charity ride and subsequent bash and bonfire. We grab the truck and make our way into town. I notice Reaper looking at me out of the corner of my eye. "What?"

"You've been standoffish lately. Are you doing okay? I know the accident made me the group's focus, but I want to make sure you know I got your back for anything.

It's as if he could sense the betrayal. I couldn't allow Frankie to use me as a pawn against my brother.

I park and hop out, and we head toward the door, "I'm good. Being the poster child, you take the pressure off the rest of us. You're the problem child." It felt good to say that and not be it. He shoves me before grabbing a cart, and I grab another. The crowd is expected to be in the hundreds; this is definitely the first of many trips.

We were casually grabbing food and talking about how much tits and ass would be on display when the thought crossed my mind to tell Reaper how bad Daisy had fallen, but that would have created a million questions, mainly why I was there. Although I wanted to reassure Reaper that dumping her was for the best and that his hatred for Frankie was justified, it exposed me.

I was grabbing the bacon for Sam's famous bacon-wrapped chipotle scallops and stuffed peppers when Reaper split off to get the cheese. I was scouting the ladies who were there doing their weekly grocery shopping when I spotted Frankie walking in with a woman and a little girl. The woman looked familiar, but I couldn't put my finger on it. I slide back into the aisle to keep Frankie from trying to pull a power move while my brother is here.

The instant anxiety had me craving a pill. They were headed toward the produce area, and I knew Reap had only gone an aisle or two over; I was safe to look. As I round the aisle with the chips, I see him lifting the same little girl to grab a bag. He seemed so enamored by her. It was second nature when interacting with her.

We all know that out of all of us, Reaper is the inevitable family man. No one has a bigger heart. I don't mind that if I didn't have this paralyzing fear of becoming my dad. That's why I'm keeping the ladies at arm's length.

Satisfied with her selection, she disappears around the corner. Reap looks back at me when I roll up, "Always helping, huh?"

"You see how tiny she was? She'd never reach her favorite bag of chips, and climbing would have been too dangerous. I was there at the right time."

"Since we're here, should we grab some?"

"I was looking for those garlic-onion pretzels for Dixie's world-renowned onion dip. She taught Lil how to make it, and she will whip up a huge batch of it." I'm glad she showed someone because that dip was out of this world. "That is the best combo, but we should get some regular chips, too." Something about them makes the combo addictive. My mouth is watering thinking about it.

We take opposite ends of the aisle for these specific pretzels. Suddenly, Reaper stops when he

hears what sounds like a man yelling. It actually sounds like...

Then, the same little girl from earlier races passed me with Reaper immediately behind her. "Watch the carts!" He tells me as he races out of the store. Now, I'm stuck with two heavy carts of food. Then I hear a woman frantically calling out before the door chimes, opens, and closes.

"I want that mangy brother of yours gone!"

I turn to see Frankie behind me, angry as usual.

"And what's that got to do with me? You got your plan, remember?"

"You're right, and I will do it tonight!" He snarled. With his mouth salivating, he walks out of the store.

I slap my hand against my forehead. Putting my brother at risk for drugs? What am I doing with my life?

Reaper is taking forever, and when I abandon the carts to see what is going on, I see him in a heated confrontation with Frankie. He looks like he is speaking to the woman now holding the little girl's hand. Reap gives Frankie one final glare before they follow him to his car.

I return to the carts as he strolls in, mumbling a string of curse words. I knew what this was, and I also knew he would not accept it for what it was, not after having his heart broken and set on fire. He shook his head, and I broke the silence. "Dude, what was that?"

He shrugged, "I'm still trying to figure it out, but that's Frankie's sister's daughter, Raven." So, the adorable kiddo had a name.

It was funny that he couldn't see it, but it was so obvious. He let his bitterness blind him to what was in front of him. I'm just here to open his eyes beyond his comfort zone.

We were unloading our carts into the truck bed when I said it as bluntly as possible: "...Look, you keep having these run-ins for a reason. Just...keep yourself open. That's all." He absorbed what I said but didn't respond. He was deep in thought.

Whether it be married like Lucifer and Sam, doubled up with two girls, or a pre-made family, I wanted happiness for all of us. I didn't know what my endgame would be. I hadn't had a steady girlfriend since Claudia in high school. I tried not to treat the girls like they were sluts, but they acted like it, and no one piqued my interest beyond a quick fuck.

It wasn't my main focus, anyway. I was here to have fun and enjoy my freedom.

Later, we settled into a movie night in the living room, where we wind down from the day. The house wasn't blaring rock 'n roll with the girls dancing on the bar. It was almost a family-type atmosphere. These moments remind me of when Mom would gather us all to watch Disney movies. She even made each of us personalized snack trays. Mine was popcorn, cheez-its, jolly ranchers, and airheads. I loved seeing her smile watching us. I found myself looking at them like she looked at us, an unwavering love.

The pick was a cheesy 80's action movie. You know, the good guy saves the girl from a monster of a bad guy. Then, 52 explosions and hundreds of bullets are shot in the action sequence, yet no one gets hit. It made absolutely no sense. This is the last time we let Wicked pick the feature. I can't believe this was popular back then. He's way too young to choose this type of movie.

The next couple of weeks were so busy, not only with the grocery runs but cleaning the house, mowing, trimming, and setting up a makeshift parking area for all the bikes, total back-breaking work. We will have earned this break to hang out with our brothers from far and wide.

I'm starting to doubt my control over my habit, but I keep convincing myself that it isn't that bad, but it could be. I haven't taken a long enough break to know the side effects of the red riders; they are the new and improved cliffhangers. Substantially stronger with possibly one drawback: even stronger withdrawal symptoms. I had to decide if I would pop my pill or skip it and enjoy Josiah's brew. There is no way I would risk doing both.

As I predicted, Frankie tried to implement his plan but failed miserably. It was confirmed when Lucifer called for church immediately after and revealed Frankie's request and probable intention. Not only is Lucifer our leader, but he's a father figure, too. He smelled the setup a mile away. I'm sure Frankie will bitch and moan, but I can deal with him.

Back to the event, we are still prepping for it while running jobs, fixing, and detailing our bikes as we lead the ride that will start at our clubhouse. It was a lot of pressure on our chapter. You wanted to be the talk of all the chapters until the next club tried to upstage you the following year. It was healthy competition.

This year, we were looking to outdo the Southside New Jersey Devils chapter, which held a baseball tournament and awarded the champions a huge trophy. If I remember from the booze-filled haze, it was the Georgia chapter. Then, the chapter rented out a regional park for a party/campout. It was almost family-style, but we were the Devil's Ignited chapter. We needed unadulterated chaos, in one word: debauchery: bikers, sex, and booze.

We decided to do the bike ride first, then a barbeque and bonfire. Then I overheard the bunnies say they'd sponsor a sexy car wash to raise more money during the after-ride festivities. I hadn't seen another chapter have one, but I had yet to hit any big city chapters past New York; that was wild. Their event ended up in a drive-by shooting from a gang that tried to infiltrate their territory. It was bold to try when several chapters had their backs. It didn't end well but we don't discuss it to avoid implication.

Besides, we were going for the most donated during the charity event. The Illinois chapter currently holds the record for raising $16,000 by doing a carnival and a private, invite-only benefit concert. I heard they paid a pretty penny for the Alister who headlined it. Given how much they spent, it counteracted the donation and then some, but that's the path they chose.

We wanted to donate as much money as possible with a low-cost celebration, and what better way than food, football, and Josiah's infamous moonshine? Guaranteed to mind fuck you for future generations to come. Reaper got so wasted one time he ended up passed out, butt-naked, on top of the truck. I laughed so hard, and he didn't budge, so I stumbled into the house, came back out with a fly swatter, and swung for the rafters. The sound echoed when it met his ass, and he tried to chase me down but immediately detoured into the bathroom. I had to empty my stomach behind the barn. I had run too far away from the house, I would have never made it, and Sam would have skinned me if I puked on the floor.

CHAPTER SEVEN

HOOKED
THE MERCILESS FEW MC: DEVIL'S IGNITED
Briarswood, Mass.

The morning of the ride, Poppy played hop-on-pop until I tapped out after round three. I'd be no good for the ride if I were physically drained. I wouldn't be able to maneuver properly. She pouted, "Aww, come on, Fiend, they don't call you that for nothing. You can't give me a taste of that wonderful dick, then take it away. That's not fair." She's starting to sound like Dixie before she left.

"We have the bike ride, and I need to get ready and prepare my bike. You can use that leftover energy by helping the girls in the kitchen."

She reared up, "And what's supposed to mean?"

I groan, "Don't even. You know I didn't mean it in a chauvinistic way. If I had, you would have been tasked to get the groceries instead of us. This is an equal opportunity house." I hope that stroked her ego so she could drop it. I grab a towel and step out of my room to the bathroom with her hot on my

heels and still naked. I stop at the door, "Sorry, doll face, I shower alone." She gazed down, licking her lips, then a full-blown grin. Wicked strolled past, and she didn't even attempt to cover up. She stood defiantly on her tiptoes and swayed her tits. "Can I at least be your backpack on the ride?" Another way to stake her claim, it wouldn't mean anything to me. "Fine, don't embarrass me. You better be on your A-game and best behavior." She hopped up and down, squealing.

She dressed and quickly headed out the door to be eye candy on the back of my bike. No doubt she'll be overly made up and underdressed at the same time. Only the ol' ladies would ride behind their men in the past, but now some bunnies get the fortunate opportunity. They think it gets them closer to permanent status, but not with me. Poppy was my guaranteed good time, but not for a long time.

After a long shower, I slipped on my black jeans and tank and finally my cut. After chatting with Sam, I finally walked outside to see Poppy...

Whoa.

Have you ever looked at someone...and fuck the shit out of them in your head?

I was doing that right now, even after this morning's fun. She is in her sexy denim shorts, with the fringe longer than the fabric itself. She paired it with a silver sequin bikini top and a black mesh crop top over it. She had to be participating in the car wash looking like this. She made one sensical decision by wearing high-top sneakers. The exhaust pipe can get screaming hot with rides like these, and if you aren't careful, you can get 'kissed by the Sun gods themselves.'

She swayed back and forth. She had a lot of faith in that

tiny triangle of fabric. Maybe the nipple piercings held some traction. I take her hand and spin her, my open hand connecting with the cheeks of her ass. It made everyone outside pause before she giggled. "Ooh," she leaned over my bike, "may I have another?"

The continued fantasy of slamming into her as she clutched my bike for dear life was clouding my rational thinking.

I shake my head. Enough of that before I have a very long, uncomfortable ride. Lucifer takes his place at the head of the procession.

He whistles loudly, "Thank you for participating in the annual Merciless Few B.A.C.A ride! The Devil's Ignited chapter and the entire northeast welcome you to Briarswood, Mass-achusetts. Now, per tradition, before any ride, we rev our engines for those who died unnecessarily and those we could not save. When we finish we rev them for those lives we saved. We will always be the hero, a haven, and a brutal fist against abusers of women and children, hear, hear?!"

A boom of 'here here' rang out, followed by the thunderous roar of our engines. After the revs turn to hums, we saddle up and wait for our marshal to start the ride. Poppy wraps her arms around my waist, slipping her hands under my cut and shirt to massage my stomach. She slides up and down slowly, methodically. Her nails scraping me sent a shiver down my spine. I rev my engine, so she doesn't hear me growl. It's a slip-pery slope if she sets off the pain. I didn't want to need it.

The ride was smooth as butter, and we ended it revving our engines, filling the air with whistles, hoots, and hollers. I got this sudden adrenaline rush, so I lifted Poppy off my bike and dipped her for a kiss. She looked surprised when I propped her back up. "Wowee." She grazed her lips with her fingertips. I noticed her lipstick didn't smear a bit. Good to know, as I let those sensuous scenarios play in my head as I push my bike into the garage before starting my assigned task.

I went into the kitchen to grab trays of marinated meat in the chest of the refrigerator for the BBQ pits. We had two of them filled to the brim, and with hundreds of hungry, voracious bikers, I would need to make a few trips before taking over one of the grills for Lucifer. We started by splitting the chicken, burgers, and links between the grills. Those were the quickest to cook. You wanted to avoid diving into Josiah's brew on an empty stomach.

The music gets cranked up. You could hear it from every inch of the property and then some. Then came the cries of the start of a good time. When I walk out with a tray, the dance floor is established, the car wash has begun, and holy shit, there are wet, soapy tits everywhere! Suddenly, I regret putting my bike away. The girls are dancing, tossing buckets of sudsy water around, but more on themselves than the bikes, and they use their soaked parts to clean the vehicles. The tip bucket is already filling up. Some bikers pull up folding chairs and watch them like it was a strip club.

"Hey, you need some help?" I look over to see Poppy's bone dry. I assumed she chose her outfit to get wet.

"You're not soaking it up at the car wash? You sure have the outfit; you might double the profit." I thought I'd throw in a compliment; I kind of like the way her eyes light up when I do.

"It's not my scene. I could help bring food or run plates between the kitchen or picnic tables.

I chuckle, "Hmph, a bunny who doesn't want to flaunt her ass in public? Doesn't that defeat the purpose of a bunny?"

Her face turned into a scowl, and she huffed, "We bunnies understand our roles and places, but we don't always stay naked or on our knees! Sometimes, a bunny is a girl who likes a boy, but you only see me as an object. You're a fucking prick!"

She stormed away, and Lucifer looked at me. I felt terrible, but isn't that common knowledge about bunnies? They were objectified, but most thrived on it, almost begging for it.

Not Poppy, it seems. Maybe I shouldn't assume.

I look at him, "I..." Throwing my hands up in defeat.

"Ahh, to be so young and stupid. Let me save the remainder of your 20s because men don't gain wisdom until they hit 30, sometimes not even then; that girl fancies you a lot and is trying to open your eyes, but you're too foolish to notice her, or maybe you're ignoring her. Whatever the case, you don't see the aftermath, but I do. I see the sadness and heartbreak every time you pick another girl over her. She's trying to respect your boundaries but won't wait forever, Jett."

I haven't heard my real name in so long; it put it in perspective if he broke out my given name. I distract myself from acknowledging what he said by trying to disseminate the smoke building up after opening the grill.

"Lucifer, I'm here to finish our discussion from our last phone conversation." I peek around the grill to see Frankie trying to puff out his chest like a gamecock and attempting to sound tough against the boss man. I observe while putting the ready food in the aluminum trays.

"Nothing to discuss. I'm not letting my boy go because you got a hard-on for him. If I remember correctly, you took his girl, and you've been throwing it in his face ever since. I'm not sending him anywhere."

Damn right! And we know he'd ambush Reaper with his security, then after they work him and he's unable to fight back, the coward would execute him.

"Do you realize I hold your contract? Without me, you and your mangy pack have nothing!"

Mangy?! He's got some nerve...

Lucifer stepped up, looking down at Frankie like a spoiled

child. Lucifer addressed the crowd about Frankie, and then they chimed in, but my attention was taken away when my brother barreled his way through the crowd to get to his sworn enemy. I buried my shoulder like a tackle, but he kept pushing forward and swinging. I took a few blows to my back. Then he shoved me to the side. I knew he was strong, but rage made him uncontrollable.

Lucifer was able to plant himself and hold him back. "Stop, Reaper, he ain't worth it!" I look past my obvious pain to help the group keep our brother out of jail.

I don't blame him; the wreck, the condition of his bike, the injuries, and his girl cheating were completely Frankie's fault. It got super-heated when Frankie's sister tried to be the voice of reason and get in between them, but Frankie pushed her to the ground, and Reap went nuclear.

I couldn't help keeping him at bay because the pain started, and I couldn't stand upright. I had to lean against a nearby tree. I returned to the grill to stay distracted from thinking about the relief in my bag. Only a few steps away...

"Are you okay?" Poppy asked as she ran her hand under my shirt to rub my back, but it irritated it more. I grimace a little, then stand straight, separating from her touch. "Get me a shot, doll face. It'll help." She nods, and I prepare a hotdog to precede my liquid medication. I pray because it's stronger than Zeus himself that it numbs my senses or calms the receptors in my nerves. I look back and see the little girl from the grocery store now by the adults. Where the hell did she come from? What is happening?!

"Fiend." Poppy hands me a shot glass, causing me to swallow the food I was chewing. I took the shot back without a second thought.

Holy fuck! I think Josiah's trying to see how many drunken bodies fit on the surface of our land. This is much stronger than any batch in the past. If this is his special occasion brew, I hope to never celebrate again.

I shook myself, "Whew, holy hell! Have you tried it?" I'm sure it'll knock her on her ass; she probably won't even take the whole thing. She pulls another shot from behind her back while maintaining solid eye contact. She tipped the shot glass, which was filled more than mine, let it pool, then swallowed with no reaction, only a smirk. I watched her throat contract, following the trail down, and suddenly I was staring at her tits.

That was the hottest thing I've ever seen. She knew what she was doing, and I was impressed.

Then Lucifer shouted for our chapter to go into the house and let the party resume. "Gotta go." Not sure why I even said anything.

The scrap between Reaper and Frankie had reached its boiling point. Observing my brother, I saw the emotional connection. His heartstrings were tied to that pretty little lady and her daughter; otherwise, he wouldn't have slammed his fist into the wall to extinguish some of his rage.

I wondered how this would affect my ability to get my pills. I could get turned away for my affiliation alone, and for a millisecond, I was angry with my brother for potentially sabotaging me. Then I worried, are the drugs becoming more important than my family? The family I sought, who opened their arms out to me?

There's got to be a better way.

"Fiend," Lucifer catches my attention as Sam switches to mama Bear mode to take care of Reaper. "Help me present the check." I followed him outside, where the B.A.C.A reps were waiting nervously in front of the dance floor. They were soaking in the 360 degrees of depravity that surrounded them. Compared to the crowd full of leather and denim, these guys looked out of place in their business casual wear. Their eyes widened as we approached, and then he smiled, "Mr. Perez, it's good to be here."

"Please call me Rocco. We are honored to present the organization with a total of $18,703; it is a record amongst the Merciless chapters. You should stick around and celebrate; I'm sure our bunnies can add to the total with their... car wash."

You could see his face go from pleased to shock when he looked at where Lucifer was pointing. The girls whistled and waved at the reps while continuing to molest the bikes.

Lucifer chuckled because they all blushed, "Come on, at least have a drink."

"Hey, boss, not the moonshine," I warned, shaking my head. He acknowledged and went behind the bar to make them a drink a little less deadly.

CHAPTER EIGHT

HOOKED
THE MERCILESS FEW MC: DEVIL'S IGNITED
Briarswood, Mass.

Meanwhile, my brain reminded me of the blows I had taken earlier. To ease the pain with one pill, it begged. I had developed a habit of keeping count, and I had ten pills left. There needed to be ten very good reasons to take them. I even stopped taking them to enhance my sex drive. In fact, when I took them for pain, I doubled down and fucked whichever bunny was available while it was still coursing through my system.

Most of the time, it was Poppy who benefited from my addiction. She always seemed to be conveniently around and dressed like she wanted my attention. Her need to be dominated always puts her at the top of my to-do list.

I whistled for her to follow me. She smiled from ear to ear

as she hopped off the back of the truck. I stood at my door, and she strolled past me, licking her lips and dragging her hand across my stomach. She slid her hands to my belt, unbuckling, and I felt it moving until it was in her hands. Instinctively, I grab a handful of hair, and she gasps. "Why don't you get ready? I need to take a leak." She pulls me down for a kiss before turning around and walking toward my bed, pulling off her top. I quickly grab my pouch and take it with me into the bathroom. I opened it to see that I only had eight pills. I forgot about the double dose to take care of Poppy and Kitty. They worked me up with their teasing and caressing of each other. After the second round, I didn't want it to end and popped a second pill, screwing into the wee hours of the morning, counting orgasms, Kitty with six, and Poppy hitting double digits with the bonus of being a squirter. I'd focus on her more to feel her cum and almost drown me.

"Shit!" I was disappointed in myself because I'd have to hit up the Dollhouse, and after what happened earlier, I knew he would blame me and charge me some exorbitant amount or outright refuse. I sigh at my circumstances. I hate to leave her high and dry. Perhaps I can persuade her to suck me off and take care of her later once I re-up.

I walk back in and shut the door to drown out the commotion of outside festivities. Poppy sits on her knees with one pillow between her legs, the other in front of her, and nothing else.

She smirks, "I already came all over your pillow. Sorry, I couldn't wait, but I was also marking my territory." She licked her fingers, which were soaked in her.

"Were you now?" She nods.

Hmm...interesting. Then, my attention was taken away by the front door slamming, but there was no yelling, so I focused back on her.

"I have a proposition for you. I need to make a run in a minute; suck me off, and when I return, I'll make it up to you."

My dick was pulsing so hard I thought the constant contact against my jeans would make me bust. I was ultra-sensitive. I was also aware of the pulsing pain with my scar; they were competing for my attention. At that moment, the attention shot to my scar; it was a solid 7/10 on the pain scale, reminding me of my past mistakes at the same time.

I didn't even notice Poppy on her knees; she sat up to unbutton my jeans, pulled everything down, and stared at her prize.

"Ooh, you're dripping wet and ready to cum. Your wish is my command." She leans in closer, her breath torturing my sensitive skin. She exhales hard, making me groan loudly. I look down, and that's when she pulls the trigger. She waited until I gave her my full attention. She works me up, and I sigh at how good she feels, especially when she tightens around me.

"Fuck yeah, that's a good girl." She pulls back slowly until I'm completely out of her mouth, saliva dripping from my cock and her lips. Her hand squeezed in a pulsing motion, but there were no words between us. The silence allowed me to hear voices. One was Sam, but the other voice sounded like a kid. None of the girls had a squeaky voice you could mistake for a child. I looked back down, and Poppy was twisting and stroking me, my knees slightly buckled, causing her to stick her tongue out.

She knew.

She stroked a bit faster, and I shot everywhere, even though she clearly wanted to taste me. She only tasted a fraction of it. I sigh in relief, "Sorry, darling." She drags her finger across her left breast, sticking it in her mouth. "No problem."

Now I hear singing and laughing; what is going on? I put

myself away. "Stay here. It sounds crazy, but a kid might be in our house."

She looked so confused and lay in my bed. "It's okay. I'll wait here so I can get what I'm owed."

I open my door at the same time Demon walks in with Wicked and Lucifer following him in. I walked into the living room and noticed a plate of mini pancakes. Demon sat down, "Sweet, pancakes! You don't want any?" He said toward Reaper while shoving a couple in his mouth. Reaper shook his head and then explained what had happened since Frankie left. Then, it went whisper quiet when a little girl came out of the kitchen with Sam. She was holding another plate of pancakes. It looked heavier than she was, but she made it to the table without spilling. I looked at Sam, who was beaming at the sight of this tiny human. Sam tells us that Raven wanted to give us first dibs because she liked us, then ushers her back into the kitchen as we get the whole story.

It's unbelievable—what she went through and what she saw. I saw the exact moment Reaper went beyond the point of no return. It was when he told us that Frankie had taken his sister from the house and left the girl.

He had to have her at the Dollhouse, probably making her do the unthinkable. I didn't say anything; I didn't want to add to his anguish or give him new things to worry about.

"Strap up." Lucifer announced, "I let the Sheriff know it was going down. When we arrive, we have 15 minutes to complete our business before they show up and clean house, so let's go!" It was the final round, and it would end in bloodshed.

I didn't know Boss had it in good with law enforcement, but I'm glad he does.

I load my holster with two.45 Glocks and slip it on under

my cut. My mind is racing because there's a good chance I could lose my supply chain.

Maybe I should; it'll be forced sobriety. Was I ready for it? No, but there was nothing I could do about it. Frankie was going to go down.

Reaper led the rescue mission, and some members of other chapters tagged along to the Dollhouse. He kicked the stand out and was already on his way in before we had a chance to park. The bodyguard tried to warn Reaper not to come in, but he decided that talking was not the answer and shot that bastard in the kneecap. His screams were filled with anguish as Reaper told him to tell his boss that we were coming. He doesn't wait and storms in; the bar immediately breaks out in screams from the girls as they run out along with the patrons. The brothers would watch for any of the staff. I slipped in and headed to the right; I knew where Frankie's office was. Demon took the left side, and we would meet in the middle. I quickly head toward Frankie's office to avoid Reaper coming in, blasting away recklessly. I open the door with my gun drawn. I hoped to catch him and make it look like he slithered away, but he wasn't there. He must have booked it when he heard the motorcycles coming; maybe he was tipped off.

I'm startled by gunshots. But before I close the door and walk back, I notice several bags of different pills. It's like they were parsing them out for the dealers to sell.

I recognized a pile of pills.

Not just any pills...

They were little white tablets with a distinct red stripe down the groove in the middle.

The ones I need...

My mouth was watering. Only an addict would think about taking them in the middle of a violent rescue.

They were plentiful and haphazardly strung along the

desk, hundreds showing recent activity. I heard furniture being thrown, and I didn't need anyone to come back here.

I haphazardly grabbed a handful and threw them in the bag, shoving them in my pocket. It was an excessive amount— like I found a pot of gold.

I slip back out and walk against the wall, always keeping it against me. Then, I cut across beside the stage, ensuring I aligned with Demon as he scanned his side. Then he stopped suddenly and pointed. Coming from the hall was Reaper's girl. She was in a bad way, stumbling in her nose-bleed heels and wearing next to nothing. Her skin looked clammy, and she struggled to keep her eyes open. Demon screams for Reaper, still pointing in her direction.

She gathered all her energy to call for him and reached out before he dove to keep her from slamming against the ground face first. Demon tries to help, but he won't let anyone near her, now was not the fucking time! Demon calls 911 as Reaper asks, but I kneel to see if I see the all too familiar signs, like my mom when she tried to cover up her use.

Another reason I despised my father. Her drug use was a cry for help, his help, but he ignored it and her. Sadly, he didn't realize his perfect model wife was crumbling due to trying to raise and keep us happy, to keep us unaware, but we knew. My older sisters and I had secret meetings about it. Dog and Kat were too impressionable.

"She waits until after dinner when Katy or I are washing dishes. She alternates between popping pills, or if it's been really stressful, she'll shoot up. She's forgotten her door was cracked open a few times." Chelsea relays what she's seen, and Katy nods in agreement. It hurt us tremendously to see our mother hurt and worse to know her solution to it all. I purposely tried to avoid it by staying out late with my "hoodlum" friends, as my dad called them. It was then I wondered if my actions were exasperating her use.

Was I to blame? Everyone else was a model child, and then I was the black sheep. The one she worried about was the one who contributed to her stress lines and gray hair. She always gave me this smile of hope that said I love you no matter what.

I shake my head to bring myself back to the present. I see one of the telltale signs and point it out, "She's inflamed..." I explain what I know, but he gets distracted when she comes to. He tries to get info out of her, like who did this to her, my money's on Frankie's little fuck toy, but then she goes limp in his arms and stops breathing! He clutches her tighter, but that's not going to save her! I had no choice but to scream at him to let me check; her pulse was super weak. I heard the sirens, but I don't think she'll make it if we don't do something now!

"She's not breathing. Lay her down...now! You want her to die?! Let me do this!" I know he knows. I mean no harm, and I couldn't fathom that little girl without her mother, especially if I could do anything about it. I check again for a sign of life, but there was none. I immediately perform CPR—one of the very few lessons that I learned that stuck from high school.

She jerks, and I immediately knew her stomach was trying to empty whatever it was coursing through her system. I turn her in time for her to throw up, and then she breathes loud and deep. She's conscious, and the sirens sound like they are right outside. Reaper looked relieved as I told the paramedics what I knew. He doesn't let go of her as they put her on the stretcher to take her to the hospital.

I can't stop shaking but walk back to the group to let them know what happened inside. Lucifer seemed particularly upset. Then, the Sheriff walks towards us. I feel anxious with these pills in my pocket.

"Evening Sheriff."

"Evening, Rocco. Let's take a walk and chat. Your guys are free to go."

Lucifer nods," Have one of the brothers from Pennsylvania take Reaps' bike back to the house." Brick, the chapter President, nods, and whistles for one of his boys to ride it back.

On the ride back, I think my adrenaline wore off, and I needed to take the edge off because what the fuck! Tonight was sensory overload in the worst way.

CHAPTER NINE

HOOKED
THE MERCILESS FEW MC: DEVIL'S IGNITED
Briarswood, Mass.

Sam and Raven were watching TV when I walked in. Raven was looking for Reaper; he held all the answers. Sam gave me a knowing look: "He'll be back after a while." She nodded while fixing the blanket covering Raven.

Raven stared at me. That little girl was bright, and I knew she could see through me. I did my best and gave her my most convincing smile. She snuggled into Sam, focusing back on the show.

Everything was up in the air. Her mother was fighting for her life. I hope my small attempt helped her improve so she could see her daughter again.

I was exhausted, and I wanted to end this godforsaken day. None of the girls were here, but I remember owing Poppy from that earlier throat job. I pop a pill; I might as well get the whole experience. I stepped into my room and sighed while pulling out my wallet and detaching the chain from my jeans.

"Ahem."

I nearly jumped out of my goddamn skin.

"Why the fuck are you in my room?"

"Shhh... I'm sure you wouldn't want anyone to walk in and see me like this."

Daisy put a finger to her lip, telling me to be quiet if I knew what was good for me. She was completely naked and perched on my bed. There was an uptick in her lips as she observed me.

I pushed the door behind me to make sure it was closed. "I said, what the fuck are you doing here?!"

She dropped the pillow, and I noticed how emaciated she was. The drugs had done a number on her. I mean, she was never my type, but she was a looker before her habit ravaged her. She lays the pillow beside her, grabbing her dress beside her. "Relax, I'm not here for that. I only wanted to see the look on your face."

"And what if Cullen walked in?" She scoffed, easily sliding the fabric up; she had no curves to glide it over. "Why would he come into your room?" She raised her brow. "Besides, we both know he ran after that dirty field rat, not even giving me a second thought! I guess it is over. Anyway, Frankie sent me..."

I shot my hand up, "I'm done. My ties with him are cut, and he's lucky he got away before one of us put a bullet between his fucking eyes."

"I'm sure your addiction says different. He sent me to give you a final assignment. He says you will do it unless you want your dirty little secret revealed." She reaches under my other pillow and produces a quarter bag of white powder. Unless she was baking a cake, I know cocaine when I see it.

"Put this in Reaper's bike. If you don't, Frankie told me to tell the cops everything I heard between you. Just because I was sucking dick didn't mean I wasn't listening." She smiled vindictively, "Oh, and

there's residue all over your bed. If they get a tip to search the house..." She didn't need to say anything anymore.

I could feel myself grinding my teeth, which caused a sharp pain down my neck to my back and over my scar. I'm exhausted, irritated, and being blackmailed by a crack whore. Now Frankie wants me to plant drugs on my brother. I guess he figured that if he was going down, so was Reaper. My brother always said Frankie would sell us out to avoid jail time. I shouldn't be surprised he'd be a stool pigeon, and we would never disclose any business dealings with him.

I wasn't going to let her leave without taking her down a peg, "You know he'll turn on you too for even one day less in jail, and you'll still never get Reaper back." Her eyes bucked; they said she wanted to scream, maybe even lunge at me, but instead, she huffed and slipped out my window.

She turns back, "Oh, and we're watching, so you had better do it if you want to keep your precious family." And like that, she was gone. I grabbed my gloves before touching the bag. Her fingerprints would be on there, not mine. But she was right about the residue; I would have to wash my bedding.

I don't know what's worse: the planting or the fear of seeing the betrayal on their faces, then turning

their backs on me. My father's voice would echo, "I knew you'd still be a disappointment. Doing nothing with your life, and look, I was right! Even the family you want doesn't want you!"

I could have fessed up, been a man, and earned their respect and trust, but what did I do? I snuck out like Daisy snuck in and headed toward the garage with our bikes. I couldn't risk it all. With Frankie locked up or fleeing for his life, it's practically over.

I looked around and behind me in case someone was wandering outside. I peeked into the garage, and it was clear. There was his Betty girl, sharp and pristine like she hadn't slammed into a boulder only months ago. The sound of an owl made me jump; usually, I wouldn't be so reactive, but I was triggered.

I took a deep breath, lifted the seat, and put the bag in, closing it lightly as if that made the deed less deceitful. I stepped out to see a dark-colored van with no lights on roll past as I removed the gloves.

Did I leave an anonymous tip about a van that may be involved in the strip club shootout headed toward the west side of town?

Perhaps.

Completing Frankie's dirty deed took me out of my mood. I tossed the bag of pills without a second thought and went to take an extended shower. I noticed Reaper and Demon had come back from the hospital and judging by the way Raven held on to him, it wasn't good. I hope she isn't dead.

The shower was soothing. It didn't entirely wash away my guilt, but it distracted me. I wrapped the towel around me and quietly entered my room. I used the extra hand towel to rub my head and face dry. I tossed it and was surprised to see Poppy in my bed.

My drug-laced bed.

"Get out of my bed, now, Poppy!" It was a whisper yell to avoid waking the house.

She looked shocked that I would raise my voice to her so harshly. She didn't move an inch, which further irritated me. She was trying to call my bluff, and I needed to remove the remaining evidence.

I pull her up and off my bed by her arm. I'll admit it's a lot rougher than I would like to be, but it was a combination of guilt and pain. I didn't know if there was any actual residue, but if there was, her body could absorb it. I'd never forgive myself.

She snatched her arm away from me, "What the hell is your problem?! I come back to get what you owe me, and you blow up like that for no reason? What is wrong with you? You know what, never mind." She grabbed her clothes and slipped them on before walking out enraged. She didn't slam my door, but she wanted to.

I didn't have time to feel. I carefully gather my sheets and toss them in the washer. I'll start it in the morning. I replace everything else with a clean set and face plant into it. I groan loudly because I know she's going to give me the cold shoulder until I apologize or grovel at her feet.

This is why I don't have an ol' lady! Being responsible for her feelings...who has time for that?! Complete bullshit if you ask me.

CHAPTER TEN

HOOKED
THE MERCILESS FEW MC: DEVIL'S IGNITED
Briarswood, Mass.

I must have fallen asleep quickly because the sun and its 28,000 watts woke me up. I checked the clock, and it was close to 8 a.m. I rolled over and was immediately reminded of last night's ordeal with Poppy. Then I looked to confirm that the bag of pills was still there and that I wasn't hallucinating. There they were, overflowing from the bag. I'm surprised Poppy didn't ask about them, but I never gave her a chance.

I stand and stretch, feeling the soreness of the charity ride, the blows from Reap, and whatever else happened yesterday. Without a second thought, I popped a pill, hit start on the washer, and went to the kitchen to grab a glass of water. Sam was in the kitchen preparing breakfast with a couple of the girls. Poppy was not in attendance. She smiles at me, and I

smile back, "Morning, Sam, everything smells good." I say as I
fill a cup with water to wash down the pill. "Morning, breakfast will be in 30-45 minutes. Hey, is Poppy in your room? She
usually helps out."

I look at the girls; if she talked about what happened, I
would know by their glares, but no one stopped what they
were doing. "Umm, no, she's not with me." She gauged my
answer, sighed, and then shrugged her shoulders, continuing
to crack the eggs. Then, we both heard a knock at the door.
Sam walked out, and I peeked to see Reaper at the door... with
two police officers.

Shit.

"Mr. Cullen Anderson?" One officer says, and he says yes.
"We got a tip that you had a large amount of cocaine. We have
a warrant to search your room and your belongings."

Reap chuckled like a maniac at the absurdity. The cop
confirmed by reading the information from his notepad. He led
them outside and, I'm assuming, to his bike. I quickly threw on
a shirt and shoes in time to see Reaper in handcuffs, screaming
how the
            charges were trumped up. Lucifer tries to reckon with the
officers, but it's out of his control.

His relationship with the Sheriff will help if the charges
stick.

The pill was starting to kick in, and I needed a release. The
squad car pulled off, and Lucifer came storming in to grab the
truck keys. Sam stops him and hugs him. His manners softened, and he squeezed her back. "Don't worry. I'm going to
straighten this out. I know a plant when I hear it."

"Bring my boy home. He's been through enough."

"I will, darlin'."

I walked back into the kitchen to put my cup away when I
noticed Kitty staring at me but not at me per se. Her eyes were

hooded as she smirked at me. Since her initiation Kitty has grown a pair and is as wild and intense as the other girls. They taught her to go for what she wants, and she has a preference for Demon or perhaps even vice versa; maybe he has an addiction to her.

But right now, she was eyeing me like she wanted a taste. I'm willing to taste a different flavor occasionally since Poppy wasn't here...

She twirls her hair, "Hey."

"Hey."

"You, uhhh...need someone to help take care of that?" Her eyes shifted south, and I followed to see the pill was in full effect. I palm myself before keeping my arm in front.

Why the hell not? "Meet me in my room. Five minutes, or I'm starting without you."

"Yes, sir." She giggled. I step out to see Sam headed back into the kitchen. She shakes her head, "Remember, there's a child in the house. Don't make me scold you like I did with Demon. No reason to be screaming like that." She huffed.

I hold my hands up, "Yes, ma'am." She shooed me away, and I stopped at my door. "You know, Sam, you make an awesome Grandma. It suits you." That made her smile so wide. She was a fantastic nurturer, especially with all of us. I don't know how she handles this much testosterone and stays so sane.

Kitty strolls out, immediately headed in my direction. She stops at the doorway; I hover over her. The shy girl who once was so timid and scared was long gone.

"You think you can handle me by yourself?" Challenging her confidence, she slid past me, but not before raking her nails across my groin. Being so sensitive, I almost lost it. I close the door and respond by picking her up and tossing her on the bed.

Just that movement and watching her undress had me raring to go.

"I'm surprised you picked me. Especially over your favorite, Poppy."

"Poppy isn't here, and I don't have favorites. I have needs to be taken care of. So, are you going to keep talking or get me off?" She motioned for me to come toward her naked frame as she sat on her knees, licking her lips.

"Mmm, your wish is my command."

"Damn right, now keep it down. There's a kid in the house."

I left Kitty panting, wrapped up in my sheets. She struggled for the tiniest bit of air after I gave her everything I had while trying to keep her quiet. I stood limp, tired, and highly satisfied at the end of my bed. Who was I kidding? That pill was a godsend. And now I didn't have to worry about supply for a while.

"Pop....I mean, Kitty, are you good?"

Whoops.

She sat up like she wasn't about to pass out a moment ago, "Wow. You're only fooling yourself, but what do I know? You were probably thinking about her the entire time."

I couldn't answer, and she didn't need one.

"See ya around." She opened the door as Poppy was about to knock. She bounced between looking at Kitty, sweaty and disheveled, then at me, who was still naked and soft. It was evident by my sweat-drenched skin that I had worked a number on somebody other than her, and I saw her eye twitch.

"Huh." Was all Poppy said before turning around.

Shit!

Kitty followed, "Poppy, wait!" And she closed the door. Usually, it would have been a tongue-lashing to rival a Jerry

Springer episode, but we've been careful to keep it decent, at least with Raven around.

I'm not going to lie; that little girl is a gem. She reminds me of what's good in this world. I grabbed a towel to head to the shower. My high was dwindling. After the shower, I was on the porch watching Raven with so much energy. She was stronger than her story and her past. That little girl is resilient.

She runs around aimlessly until she plops in my lap! "Hi!"

"Hi, are you having fun?"

"Yeah! They're building me a swing. I get to go high up in the air!"

"Sounds like fun."

"What's your name? I'm learning all the names. I know Cullen and Rocco. Oh, and Miss Sam, she's my favorite!"

"My name is easy to remember, it's Jett."

"Like a rocket? Pew!" She shoots her arms out in front of her.

"Yup, you got it right. Looks like they finished it; why don't you hop on."

"Okay!"

She hops on and immediately starts squealing. Hearing my nickname, rocket, reminded me of the twins and how everyone was doing. I admit, I want to call, but if Dad picked up, he'd have state and local cops after me.

Out of the corner of my eye, I notice movement and see the truck pull up. Lucifer and Reaper hop out, and I sigh in relief. He wouldn't spend hard time in jail, or at least not in the short run. He stooped down for Raven to run into his arms. He has the same joy Sam does when she is around.

It was hard to sit there while he was consoling Raven. Lucifer tells us that he has to go to trial and cannot leave the immediate area. So the charges could stick. Everything rides on Avi's testimony once she's well enough.

I spent the rest of the day on my bike, taking a long ride to reflect on my past and present decisions.

CHAPTER ELEVEN

HOOKED
THE MERCILESS FEW MC: DEVIL'S IGNITED
Briarswood, Mass.

After a couple of weeks, I noticed that Poppy still had yet to show up to the clubhouse. Or she was avoiding being in my presence. Kitty had been hanging around as usual, but she'd been standoffish toward me. However, she resumed her pursuit of Demon.

I caught up to him one day in the gym, "Hey, has Kitty said anything to you about Poppy?"

He raised his brow, "She doesn't say much when we play because she's gagged. But in general, no, she hasn't said anything. Why? Did they fight? You know I love a good knock-down, drag-out catfight."

I sighed, "Nah, man. There was an incident when she saw

Kitty leave my room. She didn't yell or scream; she just walked away, and I haven't seen her since."

He shook his head, "When will you and Reaper learn about the female species? You guys are like bookends, except he's finally accepted his feelings about Avi. You... you're damn blind if you can't see that Poppy wants to be your ol' lady.

"I don't want an ol' lady."

"You may not want one, but you need one, especially with our pending legal issues and our affiliation with Frankie. We're talking about serving hard time. Wouldn't you want to have someone happy to see you if and when we get out?"

"I don't see you trying with Kitty."

"It shows what you know. This isn't about me; you asked about Poppy's absence from the clubhouse. What if she's moved on to someone else? She's a beautiful girl...and a wildcat the handful of times I had her. You're probably too late." He hits me with his towel before leaving me in my thoughts.

Is that it? Did she find another guy to cling on to? A few much smaller biker groups tried to mimic the Merciless Few, down to the bunnies, but they don't stand on anything; they don't fight for the underprivileged as we do. They are useless carbon copies of our great chapter.

Could she have found someone in one of the knockoffs?

I popped a pill and had one of my most intense workouts ever. I am dripping wet head to toe, peeling my shirt off, and walking back to the house in my basketball shorts that barely cover. All my senses were cranked up to 100. I see the girls at the bar gossiping as usual, except there are two new faces. They must have recruited them and are giving them the rundown. I wipe the towel across my chest.

"Oh, this is Fiend, and apparently his chest, too." They all laugh, "He's as fucked up as the rest of our guys, not as sadistic as Demon but a close second. Fiend, meet Lacy and Rose; they moved into the bunny house a few days ago. They were prospects to be Ace of Spades bunnies, but we convinced them that we were much better, and now they are prospects to the Merciless Few." They hoot and holler in excitement.

Ooh, fresh meat, and I was on my high, but I'm sure they weren't ready yet.

"Hello, ladies. Good luck with your mission to be our bunnies. I'm sure you and I will become very close once you cross over." I see the blush on Rose's cheeks.

"Demon and Fiend like to break in the new girls. He's not as diabolical as Demon. This is a friendly reminder that Lucifer and Reaper are off-limits and taken. Wicked, you need permission from the twins to share or join in, but Demon is fair game." She pauses, which causes me to speak up, "Wait, what about me?" I made sure to brush my hair away, gauging their reactions. They exchange this look and burst out laughing.

"Be fucking for real; you're semi-available if that. You have your preference. You're like five steps behind Reaper and his instant family. If you'd get some sense..." Lila stopped, implying. She was a real hard ass, never one to mince words, but I didn't want to hear it.

"That again. I told you all I don't have a preference or a favorite. I just..."

"...have needs to be taken care of, right?" Kitty finishes my sentence. "Lil's right; you're delusional, but nobody can make you see it. Bunnies can't be bunnies forever, Fiend. Dixie found love and left." She checks her watch, "Oh, gotta go. I think Poppy's back from her date by now. I'm going back to the house to see how it went." She stopped by the bar and grabbed a quick shot from Wicked, who was restocking and shelving the glasses, before heading out.

There was no reason to say that aloud than to watch my reaction. I walked away, but my curiosity was piqued. A date? With who? The bunnies should be loyal to us and us only. But she's right; they are not obligated to be bunnies forever, especially if they have no chance of being an ol' lady.

CHAPTER TWELVE

HOOKED

THE MERCILESS FEW MC: DEVIL'S IGNITED

Briarswood, Mass.

It's been a hectic few weeks. Avi testified against Frankie. She had enough credible evidence to send him away for good, but it also implicated us when we did work those security/transport jobs. Avi tried to get us immunity, but it was a no-go. We reassured her that we had been dealing with her dirty brother long before she came here; we knew the risk, and we take our sentence, whatever that may be, with pride.

Reaper finally came to terms with his feelings for Avi and Raven. I've never seen him happier; this is what he needed.

Boss man negotiated our surrender to the police. The sheriff worked on our behalf to get our sentence reduced...and he did. We would be sentenced to six months in state prison for drug trafficking and pay a $10,000 fine. Boss said he had enough saved to cover the fine, the bills/utilities, and more while we finish our sentence. He said that was easy; relaying the news would not be.

It was only after the sentencing that Poppy showed back up. I'm sure the other girls kept her current about what was happening. The night before our sentence started, it was a very somber dinner, and all the girls were devastated. The energy was so low, and Avi still wanted to take the blame.

I ended up outside on the porch. It was pitch black, and the only light was that of the lightning bugs and the sounds of crickets and owls. I felt unsure of what we were about to experience, but I did know I was about to go through one hell of a withdrawal. I was already getting the shakes and night sweats when I slept, but that's because I was very liberal with the stash I took from Frankie's office. I wouldn't call it a bender, but I enjoyed the easy access.

I was not sure what I was going to do about the random pain. I haven't had an attack, but I took my last pill last night; they wouldn't start for another day, I was guessing.

"Hey."

I look to see Poppy standing there. She sat on the other end of the bench and crossed her legs in her favorite denim blue cowgirl boots. I remember her first night; she wore a short-sleeved white button-down tied up and short denim shorts with those boots. None of the buttons on her shirt were used, so when she tied it, it became a tight, deep V-neck. She stood at the bar with one foot perched on the gold accent that circled the bottom of the bar, sucking on a cherry red lollipop. She glanced at me over her shoulder and winked.

There was a sadness, but I didn't want to leave the tension in the air until our return.

"Poppy, I'm..."

She holds up her hand. "No, me first. I know the proper

protocol for bunnies, and I did not mean to cross it. You are allowed your fill of whatever woman you want, and I shouldn't have made it personal."

"Still, I'm sorry. I shouldn't have made you feel that way. You're a great girl, Poppy."

"I know." We share a laugh, and I pull her towards me in a hug. If I was going to go six months without a woman's touch, I wanted my last moment to be in utter peace. She wraps her arms around me as she snuggles up to me. She sighs in contempt, and I play in her hair.

Something about her makes me feel safe and comfortable. "How about you backpacking me on my first ride after my release?"

She sat up and smiled, "Really?!"

"Sure."

"If you're asking, then yes!" She kisses my cheek. My ear catches a sound that isn't the usual natural noise; it sounds like...moaning.

Poppy sits up, "Is that?"

"Yup, it's got to be Reaper and Avi since they left the house about an hour ago. Guess you can't blame them, plus it's hard to have sex with a kid in the room."

"I couldn't imagine." She ran her hand up my chest, "You want a final romp since it'll be you and your hand for six months?"

"I won't do that, especially if I have a cellmate. I'll have one helluva release when I get back."

"I call dibs." She claimed so quickly.

"Of course you do. We'll see... we'll see. In the meantime, I'll take you up on your offer; now, get your sweet ass to my room ASAP." She stood up, and I smacked her ass.

"You owe me since Kitty got an all-nighter solo. And I'll

make sure, whether you jerk off or not, that I'm the one in your fantasies."

And holy shit, she was right. I popped two pills for the marathon session. I don't think I have anything left to shoot during my incarceration; it may take six months for my body to recover.

She exhaled loudly, "Wow. You were amazing." She grabbed the water bottle on my nightstand. Passing it to me once she took her share. I finished the bottle and pulled her toward me until I fell asleep. I basked in her scent, committing it to memory.

The dreaded day had come when we started our six-month sentence. I don't know what I expected; maybe I watched too much of The Wire and Prison Break. I was ready to fight it out and mark our territory so nobody would dare mess with us, but it wasn't like that. We were assigned our cells and then shown the common area and the trade school, which was full of programs used to rehabilitate inmates.

Reaper picked the automotive program, and Lucifer took business courses to manage the club's finances better. Wicked worked in the kitchen but also spent his free time in the gym. Demon volunteered in the library and checked out what they had to offer. Then there was me, detoxing in the worst way. I was too lethargic to do anything other than my assigned duties. I chose the laundry room to mask my excessive sweating, blaming the dryer and steam presses as to why I was drenched. The repetitive movement of tossing linens in the washers and dryers kept my mind off the side effects.

One day, after Sam and the girls visited, I was folding towels in the dryer room when this guy started pulling towels to help me fold.

"Sup man, I see you got the shakes. How long have you been dry?"

I was irritated by the assumption. "What are you talking about?"

He rolled up his prison-issued Henley sleeve to show his track marks. They weren't prominent; he was in the long-term healing process. He was older, maybe Lucifer's age or older. He had reddish brown hair and a matching beard. I continued folding towels as my cue that I didn't want to discuss it.

"I get it, kid. It's hard to admit when you have a problem and even tougher to ask for help, but I've seen your group come in, and I know what you stand for. You're stronger than any substance, and I'm sure some pretty girl is waiting for you to get out." He patted my back and left me with my thoughts until Wicked came to get me so we could eat dinner together.

Days ran into one another, and soon, weeks were passing by. Every day, I celebrated 24 hours more of sobriety; also, news spread of Frankie's extradition back to South America to serve out his sentence in a maximum-security federal prison. We all know you never want to get locked up in any international prison system. Our system isn't the best, but we aren't plagued by harsh, inhumane conditions, corruption, or even murders within the walls. Good riddance is all I thought when I heard from Boss man; all my back dealings and secrets die with him.

I finally became comfortable talking to Teddy about my addiction and how my brothers didn't know, and I wanted to heal to keep it that way. From then on, he kept me inspired and on track. I found out a little about his story and how he was arrested for trespassing after hours when his sister was receiving treatment for cancer. He said he knew it was after hours, but she had been declining, and he got a gut feeling she didn't have much time left. He said he had been using drugs from the time their mom died but spiraled when his sister revealed her stage four diagnosis. Her health declined almost immediately, and he shot up in hopes of joining them sooner rather than later.

"When I snuck into the hospital and her room, I knew it was the end. The beeps on the machine were slower than usual. Her breathing was shallow, but I was surprised when I saw her eyes. She had the most beautiful emerald green eyes, mesmerizing against her once-olive skin.

She held her hand out, and I rushed over." He had to pause to gather his composure. It can't be easy to relive this moment over and over.

"Corina, I said, and a tear rolled down her face. She smiled, pulled my hand toward her lips, kissed it, and whispered, 'Live for the rest of us. You are greater than your addiction.' And then she took her final breath. I felt like I fell down a black hole as I screamed for her, and that's when the nurses called the cops before security came in. I was inconsolable, and her life-less body and wavering tone signaled my last family member was gone. When they got me downstairs, the police searched me and found my syringe and vial, and that was it. Two-year sentence and a second strike. In perspective, it's what I needed, and once my time is done, I will live my life for both of them."

"Wow, that's such a powerful story. Losing your family in such a short time must have felt awful."

"That's the problem. I was so hopped up on the drugs that I didn't let my emotions out until I got here. I never properly mourned my mother and sister until I was sober. And even though it's only me, I look forward to getting out in 14 months, returning to Appleton, Massachusetts, and settling down to a quiet life. Just work and my bike. I can't wait."

"Oh, what kind of bike were you riding?"

"I used to have a vintage burnt Sienna 1970, but I sold it to go on a bender. If God grants me the opportunity, I will repur-chase it from the pawn shop where I sold it. Yeah, it'll be Pearl and me." He sighed, then smiled. I hope he gets to reunite with her. There's nothing like the relationship between a man and his bike. I named my girl Destiny because I knew she would ride me toward my dreams.

I put a pile of folded towels in the hamper that the guards would take to the locker room. He followed suit until the cart was filled. We signaled the guards, and they took both bins. I am exhausted, and the pain is irritating, not quite excruciating. I'm stretching to try to alleviate the pain or at least calm it to keep it from going full-blown.

"I see you're in a lot of pain. Were you popping them in response to that accident you had as a teenager?"

"I'd like to say it's only for that, but it was also when I was stressed, when I wanted a marathon fuck session, or if the day ended in "y"...I convinced myself that I was still a functioning adult while high."

"So what are you going to do when you go home?"

"I don't know. With my supplier in federal custody and being deported, the problem solved itself.

Teddy shook his head, "Don't be too sure; one incarcerated drug dealer only leaves room for another to come in and dominate the area. You'll still have to work hard to continue your sobriety. Don't get laxed."

These are the words of a wise ex-addict. They rang in my ear because, although it was a small town, every drug lord became plenty successful. It was an easy-access harbor and docks, with no search and seizure requirements and no customs and border patrol. I couldn't say our police force was looking the other way; they began gathering evidence the moment Frankie popped up in town. We had an increased immigrant situation, but most only wanted a better life and worked hard for the little they had; a small number became a problem and a burden.

Boss had been working with the police detectives, and his cooperation was what made the Sheriff put his ass on the line for us. And now Lucifer was trying to figure out ways to get more legit work. We secured small business owners, but the money was less lucrative than Frankie's. With Frankie, we could split the cash decently among the group. With the smaller amounts, we conceded and put all of it in the community pot. That's why there's enough to cover expenses and keep the girls comfortable.

One day, he was in the library on the computer, jotting down information.

"Hey, boss, what are you up to?"

He pulled off his glasses and wiped his face. "Ahh, just researching the businesses around town and making a list of those who receive shipments at the docks. We may be able to take some of them on as permanent clients if we present a great case. I want to make sure you boys stay on the straight and narrow. How have you been, Jett? You weren't looking too good initially but look more like yourself now."

I hoped nobody had noticed, but of course, he saw, and I'm sure he asked everyone else what they knew. "I think I was fighting the flu bug. I couldn't shake it for a while. That's why I was in my cell when I wasn't doing my duties, trying to let my body rest. I'm better now and ready to sleep in my own bed."

"Anyone you want waiting for you in your bed?"

"The way I'm pent up, I'll need a turn from every bunny to satisfy me! Maybe twice!" I laughed almost hysterically, but Lucifer shook his head.

"Still hard-headed, I see. Anyway, please consider what you got from this experience. I will ask everyone to write it down as a record to look back on."

"You got it, boss." I knew what he wanted me to say. He and Sam are the ideal biker couple; he fawned over her, and she loved her big lug. I never saw that growing up. My dad never showed affection to my mother other than a dry peck on the cheek or holding her hand during the dinner prayer. I often wondered how we all came into existence when they barely touched each other. It had to be when he was hammered. Mom probably helped him to bed and then made her move. Or maybe he showed her some affection and made her feel wanted.

I shy away because I don't want to end up like that. Robotic and emotionless, but then I realized that by acting the way I do to avoid it, I am indeed like my dad when it comes to emotion. I keep telling myself that sex is just sex—no need to involve feelings when you're only trying to drain your balls.

Was Poppy on my mind? Of course, she was, and although I said I wouldn't jerk off, I did, and the moments with her burned into memory: her moans, her screams, her scratches across my back. The eagerness in her eyes, doing everything she could to push me beyond the threshold.

But how do I establish whatever this is?

CHAPTER THIRTEEN

HOOKED
THE MERCILESS FEW MC: DEVIL'S IGNITED
Briarswood, Mass.

The time had finally come, and we were being released in the morning. I could see the sheer joy in everyone's eyes when we had church in the corner of the dining hall after dinner. "I'm proud of my boys for bettering yourselves during your time here. You could have sat around and done nothing but feel sorry for yourself; instead, you decided to make use of our situation. Some of you learned new skills, someone got even more ripped, and I learned how resourceful my boys are. I spoke with Sam, and they are overjoyed and even planning a celebration upon our return. They will meet us outside the gates at 9 am." He once again suggested we write down our experiences while incarcerated.

Tomorrow night sounds like a night of reckless abandonment.

The release was as I expected. We gathered our belongings and processed out. Then, we were met with hoots and hollers from the girls. The second the gate started retracting, Sam was sprinting toward her man. He stops to brace for the hit. It was a sweet moment between a biker and his ol' lady.

Wicked's girls were fawning over his even more muscular physique, and Raven's little legs took her to Reaper as she screamed papa. Demon hugged the other bunnies while they hugged and kissed him profusely, except Poppy. She walked around the group from the back and stood in front of me. She wasn't scantily dressed this time to grab my attention. She wore a jean skirt, a white crop sweater, and all-white high-top tennis shoes.

She swayed as she always does in my presence, trying to get my eyes to wander down to her tits. After six months, I would stare at them even if they were in a double-knit turtleneck.

Fuck! They looked delectable. Pierced and hardened as if she teased them while waiting for me, or she was just that excited to see me.

"Hi." Her eyes wander down to our feet, and I lift her chin. Her eyes light up. "Hey."

"Welcome home." She hugged me so tight I couldn't even inhale properly. "Whoa, ease up, mighty Thor."

She looked up, and I looked down, but I was distracted by the whispering that wasn't quite low enough. We looked over to mile-wide smiles and pointing as they waited for the inevitable.

I wouldn't deny them their satisfaction as I kissed her sweetly on her lips; she tasted like the purest honey on a summer day.

She touched her lips, "Wow...that was some kiss." She smiled and blushed.

"It felt right." We all piled into the truck and a rental for the two-hour drive home.

I was up early enough to see the sunrise from the mountain range. As it rose into the sky, the view changed from dark to purple to pink. It was the most beautiful thing I ever saw. I walked Destiny out and got her ready for her first ride since I left her. She needed to warm her cold-blooded engine while I apologized profusely for neglecting her for such a long time. She started up so beautifully for me as a sign of forgiveness. I revved her for good measure; it sent chills down my spine.

After having a strong cup of coffee beside her, I went inside to take a quick leak and waited for my backpack to get ready. I know it wasn't a typical nickname or even a nickname at all, but she seemed to enjoy me calling her that.

Sam, of course, was up with Raven, looking like they were getting ready for an outing. Raven had this cute denim floppy hat that matched her floral denim jumper. I know she's a die-hard bookworm. Maybe it was a trip to the library; for her, it was like Disneyland.

Sam squeezes some sunblock in her tiny hands. "Morning, up early for a ride? Missed her that much?"

"Morning. Yeah, I've dreamed about it for the past three weeks, plus I promised Poppy a ride."

"Hmm, how sweet. I know she would love that from you."

I heard my door close, and Poppy had her hair in a low ponytail. She had borrowed one of my AC/DC shirts and tied it up, showing her belly button piercing. It wasn't the usual diamond star; it looked like a little diamond-encrusted motor-cycle. How appropriate. She wore shorts and, of course, black moto riding boots.

"You ready?"

"Ready steady!" That's new. She follows me outside to my Destiny, and I whistle, acknowledging the beauty of my favorite girl.

I hop on, and Poppy kicks her leg over the seat. I hold her knee until she situates herself. I hand her a helmet as I put mine on. I hold up the thumbs-up sign to get confirmation she is ready, and after a few moments, she holds it up. She leaned forward and interlaced her fingers.

I took the same route as the charity ride; it took us through town. After hitting the outskirts, I whip my bike around the curves at an average speed, but it still excites her like she's never been on a motorcycle before.

"Whooooo!" She exclaims as we pass a nearby smaller town. I look to see surprised faces as we slow down to adhere to the town's speed limits. Now, there were a few mouths open and pointing. I looked in my side mirror to see she was flashing her tits. I reach back and squeeze her thigh, and soon after, she's leaning against me again. Truth be told, I missed feeling her tits on my back.

She's such a free spirit with a mouth so dirty it would give the Devil himself a hard-on, which is why I'm attracted to her. She has cursed me out in one heated moment and swallowed the next three generations the next, but it's not just about the physical. She does what she wants and asks no one. If I let her, she could be the stability I need.

We pulled into Bubba's Burgers; a diner known for its amazing grilled burgers. We ate and laughed, and it was two old friends catching up. She was curious about our time in prison, but I told her to be disappointed because there were no prison breaks, riots, or shankings. No crew challenged us to the death or whatever nonsense she may have seen on TV.

"Bummer," she said before sipping her strawberry milkshake and twirling a fry in the dairy treat before placing it in her mouth. "You could have tried to make up something interesting about being locked up."

"Why?"

"Then I'd see you as a hardened criminal, a bad boy, and there's nothing sexier than a bad boy." She licked her lips before she resumed pursing her lips around the straw.

"What the hell? I am in a motorcycle gang. We conceal carry when we do security jobs, and nobody is crazy enough to fuck with us. Is that not bad boy enough for you?"

She shrugged her shoulders, "I guess that'll suffice." She looked at me and gave me a playful laugh. I held my hand out, and she took it and squeezed it. I noticed a tinge of pain from the bike ride, concentrated in my back. Somehow, her squeezing brought it to the forefront of my mind. It wasn't the awful pulsing, but it could trigger it, which worried me. I tried to lean back from our joined hands to ease the pull on my muscles. She resumed finishing her fries and stealing a few of mine. I suggested that she pour the milkshake on the fries since she seemed to like it, and she said that was gross. How that differed from what she was currently doing beats me.

"You know, Fiend, thank you for hanging out with me today."

"No problem, BP."

She raised her brow, "Did you call me backpack like a pet name?"

"What? It's different!" I tried to convince her, but she shook her head and threw a pickle at me.

"You're the worst."

We spent most of the day away from the house; she wanted to go into Anderson's bike shop to buy a vest to collect patches. It wasn't uncommon for the bunnies to represent by wearing the club patch. They had to earn it; it wasn't given upon accep-

tance into the club. One of the members had to present it
to you.

Poppy grabbed a few standard patches: one that said *biker
chick*, one that said *ride a biker boy*, a Harley Davidson patch,
and *bikers do it much better*. She arranges it so they can press it
to the vest for her. She squeals in excitement when the press
comes up, and the lady hands it to her. She lays it flat. "See,
right here is where I'll embroider my club name, and here is
where I'll put my Merciless Few patch. EEEE! I can't wait!"

She slipped it on and pranced around. "What do you think?
Hot, right?!"

I slip my arm around her waist to bring her close. I could
smell the peppermint she popped from the burger joint.
Before I could answer, the lady whistled, "Ooh wee, you sure
do make a beautiful biker couple." I drop my arm, and Poppy
jumps back, separating us. She focuses on the mirror in front,
admiring her patches, then clears her throat, "Oh, no. We're...
friends." The lady stared at us and tutted. "Hmm, if you say
so. You enjoy the rest of your day." She didn't seem
convinced.

I make sure she's suited and ready for the ride back before
hopping on. Her hands lock around me, but she moves them
up and down instead of keeping them still. I rev my engine in
response. She took that as a pass and slipped one hand underneath my shirt.

I hadn't quite completely drained my balls from the lock-
up, and last night was the first time without the pills. I
performed twice before I was spent, so I was still backed up,
and her soft hand rubbing against my abs was riling me up.

I slowed down when a signal turned red. If it were just me,
I would have recklessly blown through the lights of these small
towns that probably own one police car. Instead, I propped my
bike to wait, and she took advantage by digging her nails into

my flesh and raking them across my stomach in opposite directions.

Fuuuuuuuuck!

My eyes rolled to the back of my head; then I let it fall back to signal how good it felt. When the light turned green, I accelerated immediately. I heard her scream and saw her hands up in the air before returning to my waist.

I thought I was safe. No skin contact, just holding onto me for safety. Like she's supposed to...

Then her hands slid forward and down my thighs.

Oh fuck.

I was tucked to the left in my jeans.

She rubs me slowly...methodically.

A shudder racked my body...

I'm growing against the warmth of her hand.

I'm gripping the handlebars tight, trying to concentrate on the road. She was playing a dangerous game.

She alternates between rubbing me and squeezing me. I growl loudly before hitting another red light. She speeds up, and I rock against my seat, making sure she strokes my entire length.

I'm looking around the small town we passed earlier, where they all got a free peek at her delicious tits, but there was no one around to witness my current downfall. And now I was fantasizing about her knockers.

I can't cum, especially not while on my bike, not unless she's positioned in cowgirl and I'm balls-deep, slamming into her pussy. Just the thought...her straddling me and my bike, riding me, bouncing as I thrust up against her.

We finally make it back to the house, but she's still torturing me. I lift my visor and exhale hard, "Fuck, Poppy." She leans over so I can see her helmet in my peripheral vision. She raises her visor. "What's wrong? You're breathing awfully hard." She said sarcastically, still stroking me in full view of the house. Anyone could fucking see, and I didn't care. I'm repeating 'don't cum' in my head like a mantra.

Then she stopped. "Remember when I called dibs about draining you dry? Last night was only a couple of rounds. I didn't want to seem greedy then, but after hanging out with you all day, my pussy is soaking wet. I want you to wreck me like before you went to jail."

Shit, she was looking for a marathon session, but I was hopped up on pills back then; in fact, it was a double dose. I was literally going out with a bang! I couldn't go back to that, but I also know I can't perform like that unless I am under the influence.

I dismounted my bike, took my helmet off, and adjusted my throbbing dick. She hands me the helmet and runs her fingers through her hair before hopping off. She struts past me, "I'll be waiting..."

CHAPTER FOURTEEN

HOOKED
THE MERCILESS FEW MC: DEVIL'S IGNITED
Briarswood, Mass.

I push my bike into the shed and hang up the helmets. I was in a dilemma. I couldn't get her to suck me off again, and I already owe her one; she'd never accept the excuse a second time.

I had no plan, but she expected to be manhandled, and I didn't have it in me. I'm not saying I was terrible without it, but with it, I was a stallion.

The house was whisper quiet; it seemed like no one was around. Since our release, everyone has been enjoying their freedom. But it was almost dark; everyone would be back soon unless they planned a night out at Throttle. I double-check and listen for any movement before opening my door.

When I do, I see her place something in her mouth.

She stuck her tongue out before swallowing it.

No.

I tried to stay calm. I saw the distinctive red stripe before it disappeared. "What was that?"

"Don't ask stupid questions. You have a whole stash of them."

At no point did I go looking for them. I had been purposefully avoiding them until I had the backbone to get rid of them. I was scared that if I flushed so many, it would clog the toilet. Throwing them away, someone could discover them. I was paranoid about someone finding out, and someone did. And worse, she was using them.

I grabbed her by the throat and slammed my door, startling her. "Why the fuck were you going through my stuff?!"

She looked terrified, but then it turned into rage, slapping my arm away from her. "Don't you ever fucking touch me like that again! I missed you, okay? I'm sorry! I wanted to sleep in one of your shirts in your bed to comfort me, and when I looked in your drawer...I saw them. I was curious, so I took one. My touch felt so good that night while I fantasized about you. There were so many I didn't think you'd notice if a few were missing."

A few? How many had she taken? In reality, there weren't many. But in my mind, even if I had the original amount I stole from Frankie, it would never have been enough because I needed a new supplier now.

I fucking lost it.

"That's not the point, Poppy! Why would you take random pills? That is dangerous and stupid!"

"So, why were you?!" She was irritated by the name-calling. That same mouth also has a vicious tongue, especially when provoked.

I stop and take a deep breath. "They are for my pain from an accident a long time ago." Trying to reason with her.

She shook her head, "Bullshit! They were for pleasure. Daisy used to brag about fucking you while high on these. She said they made you last longer. I didn't believe her until last night when you were good but not great. Then I saw the worry on your face when I asked for a repeat of the night before your incarceration. Two plus two, Fiend, I'm not a fucking idiot!"

"I'm clean, Poppy. I can't go back."

She licked her index and middle finger and slipped her hand down her shorts, "Not even for me? One time?" She held up a single finger.

"It'll never be the one time; it's a slippery slope. I can't risk it."

She scoffs, "Whatever. I don't even know why I bother. I'll see what Demon is up to. I'm sure he can give me exactly what I want."

I was heated, but there wasn't anything I could say; she wanted action. She gave me a last chance before sucking her teeth and walking out. "Demon, you got time for me, baby? I'm pent up and could go for hard and fast tonight."

He peeked in my doorway and then looked at her in question. "Don't pay him any attention; he's not up for the type of fun I'm looking for, besides... I'm not obligated to anyone." She emphasized that last sentence.

He shrugged," Alright, you got first-round pick tonight." She pranced over and wrapped her arm around him. There was this smug smile before they turned and headed to his room.

By now, Reaper had purchased a home and was working a steady gig at a shop, so the house had returned to its state of debauchery. The music was blasting; Sam was seated on Lucifer's lap as he sat in his recliner reading various proposals. Rumor has it that there was an increase in businesses inquiring about using our docks since the Boston harbor was painfully slow to empty the backlog of cargo ships, and they were willing to split the transport cost by truck from here. If we strike first, we could get a lot of steady work.

I saddle up to the bar to drown my sorrows and forget what happened and what wasn't happening. I knew that, eventually, I would be privy to the sounds of the good times they were having. I was angry at myself and should have gotten rid of the pills before getting locked up. What if Raven had gotten ahold of them? That scenario was far-fetched, but it was still irresponsible of me. Also, my ego was bruised...good, not great, kept replaying in my head.

The girls were playing strip pool; that was new. I hear them state the rules. For every ball that went in, they had to take a shot. They didn't know that Lila was almost assassin-like at pool. They'd be sloshed by the second game.

You'd think tits and ass on display would put me in a better mood, but it doesn't.

I noticed Lucifer jerk and reach for his phone before walking outside with Sam behind him.

Wicked was at the bar pouring multiple shots. I sit two stools over from the twins, who are fawning over a shirtless Wicked in his cut. He leaned my way, "What'll you have, brother?" I don't answer; I just stare. I'm sure he witnessed my embarrassment. He nods and grabs the bottle of rye whiskey and three shot glasses. I was perplexed, but he did a double shot pour for each, holding one up and sliding over the other two toward me. He waits for me to tap the counter and then his glass. I comply, "Cheers to freedom."

"Oh God, Demon! Yes!" The entire place went silent, and then the girls squealed before returning to their game.

Wicked chuckles, "And a damn good time!" He takes his shot, and I zone out. Everything becomes muted and distorted.

I'm in my thoughts; the longer I stay in them, the angrier I become. If she wants someone to fuck her into oblivion, it's going to be me.

"Fiend. Fiend!" I saw a hand wave before me and heard someone call me; it was Wicked. "Are you alright?"

I took both shots, "No, but I will be." I walked toward my room and didn't hesitate to go into the drawer and grab a pill. I popped it before heading down the hallway.

Smack "Whose pussy is it tonight? Hmm, say it!" I heard Demon command, then another slap and her moaning. I kicked his door down, and Poppy screamed. She was face down, ass up, panting for dear fucking life.

"If you utter a single syllable of his name, I'll make sure you won't be able to sit for a week. Get up!"

Demon holds his hands up, "What the fuck, bro?"

"Back off!" I snap.

Poppy gathered her clothes and held them against her body as she walked past me. I followed her, "I'll buy you a new door!" I screamed.

As I pass, I look out into the common area. Everyone is looking back at me, but no one says anything. Lucifer and Sam are still outside and missed the melee. I continue to my room. She is perched on my bed and doesn't know how to react.

I shut the door softly, "Did you enjoy that? Having another man slamming into you? Coaxing you to say his name..."

She sat back, "You weren't going to ruin me, so I found someone who could." She smirked, further pissing me off.

I stand at the end of my bed, unbuckle my belt, and let my pants drop. My dick sprang up before resuming its hardened state, pointing north with a slight curve. Again, I was leaking pre-cum not only due to the pill but also hearing her with Demon.

I stared her down, "I am going to erase everywhere that

bastard touched you. Congratulations, your little disobedience got you what you wanted."

"But I thought..." I saw a crack in her demeanor, a slight moment of guilt, but I made the decision, even if it was out of jealousy. I was in control this time.

"Never mind what you think. Are you going to put in the work, or do I need to call in Kitty instead?" I, too, knew how to push her buttons, asking for Kitty alone and not tag teaming so she could still participate. Her eyes narrowed, and she sneered while finally moving forward. When she was close enough, I tagged her ass on both sides, erasing Demon's dirty work. I know his behavior.

There was no doubt we were both acting out our emotions of anger and jealousy while I was simultaneously trying to hide my feelings for her. She wanted the title, and I hesitated. She used that against me to justify fucking my brother. Or at least she started to. I would not stand by and let him mark her like the others.

Poppy was different.

I was proud, damn near arrogant, that I fucked her sweet little ass until the early hours of the morning. She got so many rounds until I came for the fifth and final time. It seemed like her orgasms were back-to-back. I couldn't keep count. Only one side of the bed was dry for us to sleep on.

Between the second and third rounds, Lucifer yelled through the door that he was meeting with a potential new employer. The fact that it was past midnight makes me assume it's not as legal as it should be. I trust Boss Man   to make decisions for the group; whether or not it is entirely legal is none of my concern. He does have an in with the Sheriff, but we shouldn't abuse our privilege. They could still toss us in jail for breaking the law. We all agree that six months was more than enough. That's all the street cred we need.

I looked over and saw that she was still sleeping hard, strategically wrapped up in my sheets, only covering her most intimate parts, but there was still so much skin. When I stand, a sharp pain shoots down my back and to my scar simultaneously. It brings me to my knees and has me clutching my chest; it has been a while since my last attack. Looking back, it had been four months because it took me two months to detox with the headaches, night sweats, and almost crippling exhaustion. Trying to perform my assigned duties was hell when I wanted to lay in the fetal position all day. The worst was suppressing the trembling when I was around my brothers. I constantly complained about how cold it was and that maybe my iron was low, or I was coming down with something and couldn't shake it.

I grit my teeth and use the bed to get back on it. I lay back down, and the movement caused her to burrow into me. She mumbles as I scratch her scalp. She's still asleep, but her face has a distinctive smile.

This feels...nice.

CHAPTER FIFTEEN

HOOKED

THE MERCILESS FEW MC: DEVIL'S IGNITED

Briarswood, Mass.

For the next two months, we delivered/passed off shipments for one of the larger shipping yard companies whose shipments were coming from South America, taking advantage of our open dock instead of waiting in Boston. We had doubts until Lucifer told the owner about our history with Frankie. He understood, and from then on, he let us check out the inventory. We wouldn't move an inch until we cleared all shipments as legitimate.

One night, we passed off a shipment to our Merciless chapter in Connecticut. The club President, who goes by Sinner, looks like a mountain bear; he's massive compared to Lucifer. His bike was custom-made to hold his size.

They shake hands, "How's it going, brother?"

"Pretty good. I'm trying to stay on the up and up after that short stint in the pen, keeping my boy's noses clean."

"I heard about that from Dozer here." He pointed behind him to his point man and vice president. "So, which one is Reaper? The one who took out Frankie, the fucking fat ass." Everyone had a good laugh at the accurate description.

"Ayo Reap, raise your hand, son." Reaper raises his hand as he leans forward against his Betty girl. Even in the dead of night, people were in awe of her beauty; she was truly unique. I can't wait to be able to do the same for Destiny.

"Nice job and sweet bike, kid." He nods in response. "Rocco, let me ask you a question because rumor has it that there's a new drug lord, not in your town but nearby in one of those sleeper towns. And after your situation with Frankie, I thought I'd ask. He's looking to re-flood the market. He's searching for security details to get his product far and wide as quickly as possible. If he hasn't found you, he will since he knows we have a chapter near him. He's already contacted us to cover our state; the pay is good, Roc. And you know, we run our state, not the cops. I'm not saying to get another strike, but it is substantial. Way more than Frankie."

He rubbed his beard, "Hmm...good to know. Thanks for the heads up." They shake hands again before he passes off the manifesto, and the truck driver gives the thumbs-up that our part is complete. Sinner and his guys surround the truck, rev their engines, and are on their way through their state to its final destination somewhere north of New York City.

Lucifer turns to us, "Have you heard about this new drug lord nearby?" Everyone shakes their head except Wicked, who raises his hand.

"Umm, apparently, it's some guy from Cuba or has Cuban

roots. I have yet to see him, but the rumor is he works out of Cloverton, but he might be buying or have property in town. As far as I know, he has no affiliation to Frankie whatsoever."

"Good."

"Oh, I heard he has some primo stuff. I wanted to see what he might have for endurance because these girls are going to be the death of me. I blow my load in one, and the other works me up again to get their turn! It's a beautiful dilemma."

He laughs, but Lucifer groans, "You're grown men, but you know how I feel about drug use. It compromises the team if you're all hopped up."

It felt like a spotlight was aimed at me, making my throat dry. "Alright, Devil's Ignited, let's head home."

I'm conflicted. I'm relieved and upset that there may be a way for me to get my fix.

But first, I would have to figure out where he was headquartered and, more importantly, who he was. I went to Throttle to get some info but was horrified when I saw Mickey behind the bar.

You've got to be kidding me!

I guess they couldn't charge him with anything that could stick, or he squealed himself into a plea deal; that sounds like Mickey. He was like a ghost from my past haunting me—a ghost who knew too much. I look up, and he has already set his eyes on me with this slimy smirk. I grit my teeth and walk toward the bar. As usual, he's cleaning glasses.

I think that's all he does.

"I should have known we'd run into each other eventually. How's it been going for you, Fiend?"

"What the hell do you care? Scotch, neat." He stared at me momentarily but then placed the glass he was cleaning right side up. He grabs a limited-release scotch that costs $50 a shot.

I set down the exact amount, and he took it. I reveled in that moment when he noticed I did not tip him.

"So what brings you in? Are you looking for info on the new kingpin?" He raised his brow, and I'm sure I failed in not making a facial reaction.

"What makes you think that? What if I wanted a drink?"

"You have a clubhouse with a fully stocked bar. If this is your favorite brand, I'm sure you keep it in stock. Don't act stupid. You're not the first of Frankie's...fans to come in, and you won't be the last. I'm surprised you lasted this long without him at the rate you were going."

He's exaggerating. I had it under control. He sets down another shot, "On the house." But it wasn't. He was willing to give me that information but for a price. I reach into my wallet and hold up a crisp $100 bill.

"Your integrity will determine how to proceed." I tip the bill forward, and Mickey takes it and shoves it into his shirt pocket. "I told you it was on the house."

So much for integrity.

"The new guy's name is Sebastien Aviarro. He's building his empire in the next town over, but he already has employed all of Frankie's workers who weren't tossed in jail...including yours truly." He smiled and was so proud to be under the thumb of another criminal.

"Then what are you doing here and not there?"

"Re-collecting the old clients to include those who wish to remain anonymous..." He tapered off. "It looks good in the boss's eyes when I bring him in lots of business. Maybe he'll promote me from lackey to company man. Or maybe I can run this place since he owns it now." I openly laughed in his face. He glared at me, "Remember who needs who. I still keep your candy on me; I had him recreate the design and everything because I knew you'd be back. They might be even stronger than Frankie's batch." He swings the tiny Ziplock full of pills, and he's right; they look the same. My ears perked up when he said they might be better than the ones I had, but I couldn't look desperate.

He smiles as he stuffs them back in his pocket. "I'm here every day except Tuesdays and every other Thursday. I'm sure I'll be seeing you soon if you're not ready to order right now." I looked around to see if I saw any familiar faces that could place me here talking to Mickey, especially knowing his past relationship with Frankie; it would be hard to explain. Luckily, it was the middle of the day and quite desolate. I turn and leave without another word.

The next day was a not-so-good one when everything seemed to come down on you all at once. I was wracked with guilt and remorse for such a knee-jerk reaction to Poppy screwing my brother. I could have done better, but my ego got in the way. I sat in the living room with my beer while the fellas worked out in the gym. Demon didn't seem too bothered, but he said I had better replace his door or else. He said that even though having an audience wouldn't bother him, he still needed his privacy, or he'd charge us pay-per-view.

I found myself perplexed as I continued to squeeze my hand because the pain had shifted from my back to my hand whenever I made a fist, and it didn't make any sense. It was torturing me to find relief, and I refused, so I was irritated.

I heard some rustling coming from the kitchen. I thought it was Sam pulling the stuff together for dinner. I didn't have the energy to investigate, so I continued to be confused by my pain.

Then a pair of legs are in my peripheral. Poppy holds out her hand towards me, "Let's go."

"What? No, I'm not in the mood to socialize."

"It wasn't a question. Now, and carry this." She swings a basket into view. I knew if I said anything other than yes, she'd light my ass up, and I already felt like shit.

"Fine. What's in here?"

"Food." She walks past me.

"Wait, we can't put this on my bike."

She heads over to the keys by the door and jingles the truck keys. "I know. I asked Lucifer to borrow the truck. He said maybe I could get you out of your head for a while."

Lucifer watched me before he followed the others to the barn. He didn't utter a word; he wasn't one to pry, but I knew he was concerned.

We walk toward the truck, and I cross behind her to open the driver's side. "Nope, you're riding shotgun today. You don't even know where we're going." She had me there. I relent and go to the passenger side. I slide the basket in and climb in.

Her shorts are even shorter, resembling underwear, but with her cowboy boots and fringe halter, it worked for her. The sun was setting, and the rays made her look radiant as she started up the old girl. It coughed and sputtered, then roared to life. She was due a tune-up and judging by all the additional training he had learned while locked up, Reaper would take that task. He practically put Betty Girl back together himself. All the shop had to do was run diagnostics and confirm peak performance. Then he had her repainted. You could see this calm about him when he fixed her, even on difficult days.

"Listen to her purr!" Poppy joked as she put her in gear. We jerked a bit, and then we were on our way. We passed Main Street, where everyone gathered. Whether it be to grab groceries, shop, or let the kids run wild in the splash pad, you were sure to see familiar faces. Once we passed the city limit, I was curious.

"Are you trying to kidnap me?"

She stares ahead and chuckles, "If I wanted to, I'm pretty sure I could. I'm getting you out of your big head and showing you a place that's been my escape all my life."

Briarswood and its surrounding areas are known for miles of winding roads with lush forests that break away to showcase the mountains, the countryside, or the ocean. You never know what beautiful scenery you'd be blessed with. Because I wasn't driving, I was able to appreciate the views.

Finally, she pulls into a long dirt road. At the end of it, I can make out this vibrant robin blue house, which is a long way from where we were.

"Hey, this is someone's property. We can't be here." I can imagine explaining to Lucifer about getting arrested for trespassing on someone's property. She stops right before the white door of the garage and pulls the ignition keys.

"Relax."

She hops out and slams the door; it sounds like a bomb went off, or maybe I'm exaggerating because I'm on a stranger's land. I don't know if I'll run into the suburban dad or the redneck with a 12-gauge shotgun. Either way, to them, I look like a vagrant ready to rob their house. They're probably calling the cops as we speak.

I didn't realize she was on my side of the truck, "Come on."

"Poppy..."

"Don't worry, this house belongs to my family, but no one lives here. The surprise is out back now. Come on!" I open the door, and she holds her hand out. I grab the basket and follow her lead.

As we're walking, she takes a moment to look back at me and then smiles. "You know, Fiend, it's okay to ask for help or have someone listen to all your problems. Sometimes, talking it out can help. I can't believe I'm telling you this, but I watch you, Fiend. A lot. I know it might look creepy sometimes, but I wonder who you are, not as Fiend but as Jett, the person. I know I'm not supposed to call you by your real name, but our connection makes it okay. I hope that I'm right." She's right; a bunny can only use first names when granted and she's had my back for such a long time without the promise of a title; it's the least I could do. I agree, and she sighs in relief.

"I've come to know the biker with a tough exterior in front of his brothers and the bunnies, but what about those moments when I catch you thinking? In deep thought, your dark eyes soften, but then you catch yourself and try to use booze as a distraction. What about your life before the Merciless Few? Your family? Your friends? You see that right there; you get this frown line when your past is mentioned. I hope one day you can tell me. Today, I wanted you to see where I used to go when life got hard. I was born and raised in this house, and this was my oasis."

We round the corner to the backyard, which has a small lake. There's a little floating dock for jumping off of, and beyond that, a grove of sunflowers before the forest line. It's something you see in the movies, where the kids escape a harsh world to frolic and find safety amongst the flowers.

"Hey." I look down to see the blanket laid out and her sitting down. How long had I zoned out while taking in this beautiful view? She pats the empty spot next to her. I sit but don't put my boots on the soft, pink blanket. I chuckle at the contrast of my black clothes and boots against the softness. For a moment, it's just us in silence, and then my ears find the chirps of birds and other sounds of nature. I see ripples in the water. Is it from the gentle breeze, or is there some ferocious creature in there waiting for its next meal? They haven't proven that the Loch Ness monster doesn't exist.

It's absurd, and it makes me laugh. I look over to see Poppy watching me, and now I know she's just wondering what's going on in my mind. Because we're so close to the edge, I take a rock and chuck it as far as possible to see if something comes out of the water. I throw three more before she grabs my hand, "Nothing's coming out of the water. You're scaring the fish. There's some pretty tasty crappie and trout in there." I raise my brow in question. "My granddaddy planted fish there so we could come out back and catch dinner. It was a Sunday tradition to fish with Grandpa so we could have this big fish fry. I think there are some catfish in there, too." She wiggled her toes while the wind blew, her nails painted black, red, and white like our patch colors. I'm amazed at the dedication.

"We should have brought fishing poles. Wicked is an avid angler. He and Lucifer get up at the ass crack of dawn to fish at Cedar Lake."

"Next time. Right now, I want you to enjoy the peace and serenity. Nothing else matters, not your problems, sins, or whatever negativity plagues your heart."

She places her hand on mine and smiles. All the bad didn't matter to her. I had to know, "Why me?"

She looked confused, but then she shifted to sit close and face my profile.

"Why not you? I can't answer that except to say that my heart beats a little quicker when you're around. My heart breaks a bit more when you pick someone else for the night, and my mind conjures all these scenarios that include you. I can't make you see what I see, but a girl can dream, right?" She shrugs her shoulders as she shifts back to enjoy the scenery of the lake.

Her words were powerful and poetic, and she could sum it all up so eloquently. She opens the basket and hands me half a sub sandwich. It's ham and turkey with mustard, mayo, lettuce, and olives—my favorite combo. I never worry about sharing when I make it because all the guys hate olives. Only

Sam and I indulge; she usually buys a massive jar for her and me to share.

When Poppy took a big bite of the other half of the sandwich, I didn't have to wonder if she liked olives as much as we did. She grinned with a mouthful.

"Tasty?"

She managed to get it down: "I always wondered because you seemed so proud of your sandwich, and everyone looked disgusted. Have to say, it's not half bad." She took another bite, and I finally bit into mine. It's almost as if she took notes about my sandwich-making; it was perfect.

"Did I do good?" I took another bite, then leaned over and kissed her cheek. Her mouth was full of food, and her cheeks blushed red before I leaned back. "You did, kiddo. Thank you for this."

"You're welcome."

We ate silently; eventually, Poppy laid her head in my lap as we continued talking and discovered that we both share an obsession with green apple Jolly Ranchers wrapped in a cherry airhead.

She's only two years younger than I am, but unlike me, she's an only child, but she made up for it in cousins. They totaled 11, with her being the youngest girl. They nicknamed her Runt. They hung out like siblings; that's probably why she's rowdy and rambunctious, to prove she isn't just a girl. She said she always loved motorcycles, and her first boyfriend was part of the Ace of Spades, a local syndicate, where she first became a bunny.

Then she briefly touched on that time, which wasn't all roses. "The final straw was when he tried to forcefully 'share' me with his brother. I stood my ground and refused. I thought he would understand that I wanted to be loyal and genuinely loved him, that I'm not like those sloppy girls who did anything with anyone. I've never been that type. If I share or am shared, it's because I want to." It made sense; she would always ask or offer if I picked someone else.

She sipped her soda, "He didn't like my 'disobedience'...and...he hit me, gave me a real shiner. That's not what hurt the most. He forced me to watch him fuck another bunny. Not just any girl either, but the one bitch he knew I didn't like, and I'll never forget her grin from ear to ear, finally getting what she wanted. That's when I knew he didn't love me or care. I was nothing more than an available piece of ass, ready at his will. He knew he could emotionally manipulate me into doing what he wanted. For that, I had to leave. Oh, and of course, the abuse. That's why I have this cut scar on my cheek. I was young, in love, and stupid."

I'm close enough to see it when she points to it. I grab her face to get a closer look. It's the shape of a crescent moon, but that's not a cut—it was a gash when it was created.

That coward motherfucker!

I'd break his face with my fist if he hadn't left for Montana. Some family business bullshit he had to attend to. Good goddamn riddance if you ask me. Do you know how hard you have to hit someone to produce a gash like that?! My entire body flushed in white-hot anger.

She said she met Lucifer the night of the incident at Throttle. He saw the cut, doted on her like a dad, and took her to the clubhouse, where Sam cleaned her up. She opened up to them about the situation, and they told her that our clubhouse might be a better fit for her if she liked it. And she's been loyal to the Merciless Few ever since.

And I'm glad she's around.

"And what about you? What's your story? Not in entirety, but maybe a small preview." Her fingers were super close together to show she only wanted the bare minimum. Something calming about her eases my apprehension to talk about my past.

"The reason I'm here is because I fled from my hometown. The cops were going to lock me up after I was DUI and wrapped my car around a pole. That's where I got this gnarly scar from." She's seen it before, but not this close.

She gasped, "So that's how it happened. I always avoid touching it when I'm riding you; it looks like it might still hurt. On another note, thank goodness you're even alive!"

"Yeah? Not to my old man. It was another mistake from his failed son, a black mark on his upstanding reputation in the community. Especially when I refused to work myself to death in a mill and neglect my family like he did. I never wanted to be an emotionless deadbeat like him. My mother put on this perfect wife, perfect life facade, but I knew she wanted him home instead; she put on a smile and her apron to cater to us. I owe her the world." I paused, wondering what she was doing at this very moment. I know she was thinking about me.

"Your mother sounds amazing. She kept her family together despite the circumstances, putting her children first. You should go back and show her what you've become."

I scoff, no way, but she grabs my hand. "I promise you; a mother's love knows no boundaries. She only wants to see her son again; nothing else will matter. Think about it."

She leaned against me, sighed, and took my hand. She traced random patterns while I reminisced. When the tracing stopped, I looked over, and she had fallen asleep. The sun was almost gone, and she was starting to fall deeper into sleep. I put everything in the basket and pulled her to standing before lifting her off her feet. Her hand brushed against my scar, sending a tingle all over. She barely moved when I placed her in the passenger side seat and put her seat belt on. I closed the door, retrieved the basket, and shook the blanket of grass and dirt. I took a moment to watch the sun dip below the horizon. I gently started the truck up, and it rumbled to life. Poppy shifted and leaned against the window, rubbing her arms. I lay the blanket on her, and she slides until she's against me, snuggling under the blanket. Her eyes were still closed.

The drive was slow, trying not to jostle her too much. Just when I thought she would awaken, she sighed and pushed further against me. I lifted my arm and wrapped it around her shoulder. After twenty more minutes, we finally reached the house. I turned off the truck and pulled out the keys. That's when her eyes met mine: "What happened? Where are we?"

"Back at the house. You fell asleep."

Her arms stretched as far as they could in the cab, "I must have felt safe. I never fall asleep fast and hard like that."

"Why is that?"

She rubbed her arms. I could tell she was pondering how much she should reveal. "Umm, I don't know if you know that all the bunnies stay together like you do, but in unsafe surroundings. One time, I woke up to a drunk guy in my room. Anna's, one of the Aces of Spades whores. Being a bunny here taught me the difference between a bunny and a whore. Anyway, I was lucky, for him, not so much when he was looking down the barrel of my 9mm, which I keep under my pillow. I promised I would send him to the Lord's gate with half his fucking face if he so much as touched me. A girl's got to be ready. Anyway, I don't feel safe after that incident like I do here. That's why I hang around the clubhouse and hope to get chosen. At least I can sleep in peace."

"Has anyone...touched you?" I tried to hide my rage.

"Nah, I'd go down in a blaze of glory before I let that happen, especially after Bryan hit me. You don't have to worry about me; even now, I'm always locked and loaded." She reaches into her boot to pull a switchblade that she maneuvers easily. She laughs a bit, but I'm not. She senses my irritation.

"No. Don't spoil a good day. I'm okay and glad I could get you out of your head. Let's see what's going on inside. Bet you twenty bucks someone's tits are already on display."

Now, that made me laugh. I wasn't going to take that bet because she's probably right.

CHAPTER SIXTEEN

HOOKED
THE MERCILESS FEW MC: DEVIL'S IGNITED
Briarswood, Mass.

We walk in, and Demon gets my attention immediately, "Hey, we got a job with the new Frankie in an hour."

I look at Lucifer, who nods while finishing his cigar, "Allegedly, he stocks hospitals and medical centers with supplies made in Cuba for a fraction of the price. I clarified that we would only deliver his medical supplies and check the order thoroughly. Let's go, or we'll be late."

We pulled up to a dingy apartment complex on the east side of Cloverton. Judging by looks, this is definitely where a drug operation would reside. But to our surprise, there weren't apartments inside; the place had been completely gutted and resembled what the inside of an office would look like. The apartment was a facade. The outside looked like it had a film of grime that would never come off, but the inside was a sleek corporate landscape. We followed one of the guardsmen to the second-highest level of the building. There was an open-concept area with an office surrounded by glass.

Everyone is looking around but also on their toes. Even though we are meeting for the first time, this has the potential to be an ambush. He must trust us even though we are all strapped.

"Stay vigilant, men," Lucifer says, as if tuning into our feelings. The tall, lanky man opens the door for us, and we step in.

"Ahh, the Merciless Few...*Bienvenido!*" (welcome) Then the chair behind the desk turns, and we're face to face with, "Sebastien Emmanuel Aviarro." He signals toward the lone chair in front of his desk. "*Por favor.*" (Please) He insists, and Lucifer sits.

Sebastien gives us all a once-over, chuckling when he looks at me and then returning to his welcoming host demeanor. "As I said before, I need security for my shipments. Because of my ...side gig...people attempt to steal mid-transit. They destroy the entire shipment looking for...other things! I'm losing business, and these medical places are being punished."

"Well, Mr. Aviarro, might I suggest you focus your business on one or the other to avoid such terrible incidents from happening?"

Sebastien smiles while offering Lucifer a cigar. He must have done his research because Boss man gladly accepted it. Lucifer was a connoisseur of fine cigars; he had sampled them from Ecuador to Cameroon, but nothing beats the quality or taste of a good Cuban, and he always told us that.

He leans forward and takes one. "Please, take two; I have plenty from my home country. Perhaps if this contract is lucrative, I could always ensure *Senor* (Mister) Lucifer celebrates every successful delivery with a fine *Cubano.*" (Cuban)

He quickly grabbed a second before leaning back into his seat.

Sebastien stands up, walking behind his desk. "About discontinuing one of my services, I am a man who supplies the cure, whether it be materials or...medicinal. Who am I to judge?! The afflicted should be allowed to choose their path toward healing. I merely provide diverse options. Anyway, let's talk about legit business. I have steady shipments from Cuba; depending on the weather, they arrive in the second half of every month. I need you to secure the payload and deliver it within 24 hours of arrival, no matter what."

Understandably, Lucifer raises his brow, "That seems very odd for the distribution of...medical supplies. I made it very clear, Mr. Aviarro, that we are securing and delivering the medical supplies and nothing more. I will not put my boy's freedom in jeopardy."

His hands shoot up, "Understandable, understandable. You have my word, *Como un hombre.*" (as a man) Finishing with the scout's honor hand signal.

He couldn't think that we would believe him, could he? But business is business, and we would inspect each truckload with a fine-tooth comb. He sits, prepares his cigar before lighting it, and offers the cutter and lighter to Lucifer.

He holds up his hand, "No thanks, I finished one before getting here."

He agreed, then inhaled deeply, exhaling in delight. "Nothing like it. Shall we shake hands to solidify our agreement? You, the Merciless Few, will secure and guard my shipments from point A to point B. Each completed job will garner you $10,000."

Holy shit, that was double what Frankie offered. Luckily, we lived semi-rural, and expenses were nothing compared to median-sized cities. We usually pocketed most of our share after 10% goes into the club fund, but this was a game changer. It would skyrocket me toward purchasing my dream bike or at least gifting Destiny a sick paint job.

I swear Sebastien keeps glancing my way, but perhaps that's me keeping my eyes open and my head on a swivel. Lucifer stands and shakes his hand.

"Good, good, we are in agreement. Please introduce me to the team."

"Certainly, this is Wicked, Demon, Reaper, and Fiend. These are my boys."

He came over and shook everyone's hand. He shook my hand, "Fiend, huh." I was the only one whose name he spoke; again, he gave off something I didn't care for. His smile was deceitful. He stepped back, "It was nice to meet you, gentleman. I will ring you when the next shipment arrives. Please," He signaled toward the door, and we filed out.

Demon puts his hand on Lucifer's shoulder, "What do you think about Senor Sebastien? Do you think he's another Frankie hiding behind his charm?"

"It's tough to say. I don't want to assume, but I want you to come to me immediately if you see anything shady. I will not put your freedom on the line again." Lucifer, burdened by the guilt of getting us locked up, even after we declared that we do everything as a family, including incarceration. We think it makes us more badass, but all he sees is the creation of our criminal records. I don't know about them, but my record was already established. Our unity and shared guilt keep us together, even in the darkest of times.

We ride home and park our bikes. I focused on the back pain from the ride. I often wonder if there will come a time when I won't be able to ride due to the pain. What will become of me then, and what good would I be for my family?

The cure, my quick fix, is still in my drawer. I notice Reaper stretching. "Hey, Reap, can I talk to you before you head home?"

"Sure, Avi and the kids should be asleep by now. What's good?"

"Do you still feel the pain from the crash? How do you deal with it?"

"Well, mine was mostly external with the rash," he said, shifting to show me the almost healed rash; it had been a long recovery. "Of course, there was pain and soreness. I took over-the-counter meds. Avi also helps me with massages from time to time. Which reminds me, I'm due for another one cause this ride was a bit rough. You'd think they'd fix these piss-poor roads. Why, what's up?"

"Nothing, just curious. I've been thinking about my car accident injury from long ago and how it still affects me. You ever think it could keep you from riding permanently?"

"This? Nah, if I had crashed into something or was on my bike when it hit that boulder and sustained broken bones or internal injuries, maybe. Even if it did, I'd ride until my wheels fell off. Merciless Few forever, brother." He slapped my back and headed towards his car. Every family man has to have one. His stride is slow, indicative of how we all feel. I watch him reverse out of the driveway to his place that's only a few miles away.

I'm super hungry. I hadn't eaten since the picnic with Poppy. I beelined to the kitchen to get ready to make a big meal.

"Before you go tearing up my kitchen, I made burgers and fries for you guys and put it over there." Sam points to the counter by the fridge. It's the most glorious burger bar with every possible condiment available.

"Sam, you are the best mom ever!" I start to make my plate,

piling all the sides on top. I turn around to see Sam staring at me, observing.

This is awkward. I bite my double cheeseburger to muffle the silence.

"Tell me something, Jett, because out of all of my boys, your story I know the least about, and I don't pry because it is none of my business, but the fact that you called me mom makes me wonder about yours and why you don't call her."

"Sam..."

She holds her hands up, "A woman knows when a boy needs his mom. You may have been with us for a few years, but I see the sadness. I think you don't allow Poppy to be closer because of an unresolved issue with your mom." She approached me and hugged me, kissing my forehead, and I felt ten-year-old me try to stop the lump forming in my throat.

"I need to say this. I don't know why but call your mom. Tell her you're okay; ease an old woman's heart. She wants to know her boy is alright."

But I'm not. I've been dependent on medication since the accident I caused and have failed over and over again to quit. I ran away from home; I'm technically still on the run. She wouldn't rat me out, but what if my dad answered? He won't hesitate to turn me in, but Sam has never led me wrong. She's right, and I need to ease my mom's mind.

First thing tomorrow.

CHAPTER SEVENTEEN

HOOKED
THE MERCILESS FEW MC: DEVIL'S IGNITED
Briarswood, Mass.

The next day, I woke up super early before sunrise. I usually do that when something heavy is on

my mind, and since talking to Sam, my mom has been. I get dressed and grab the burner phone we use for business; that way, it cannot be tracked. The air is cool and crisp outside; it causes me to take a deep breath. I walk back toward the field, taking in my surroundings as I go deeper into the forest. Soon, I'm in the open field, looking around. I forget how stunning the still views are from the ground level and not zooming past them.

I exhale loudly as I stare at the black phone before swiping the screen, lighting it up to the default screen wallpaper. I punch in the house number hoping she never changed it. She was a creature of habit, and I hoped that would work in my favor.

My hands shake as I punch in the last four digits: 6,5,9,3; the screen flashes, and I hit the speaker phone icon that lights up, and I hold my breath. The first ring makes me jump; I don't know why.

Then another.

And another.

I started to think that it wasn't meant to be, that she had moved on and was busy taking care of Kat and Dog, who were growing up fast.

click

"Hello?" It was a female voice, but not my mother's.

"Hello?" They asked again, and I had to say something, or they would hang up. They might not answer another call from this number.

"Umm, hi."

"Who is this?"

I felt myself choke up. This wasn't my mom.

"This is Jett, I was looking for my mom..."

"J-Jett? Is it really you?" Then I heard crying coming from the female voice. "It's me, it's Kat."

She sounded so grown up. "Kat? Oh my god."

"I can't believe it. I told them you would call!"

"Where's mom?"

"I, uhh...wait here. Katy! Chelsea!" It sounds like she put the phone down and went looking for someone, but she didn't specifically call for Mom.

"Yes, it's him, I know his voice!" I heard the voices getting louder.

"Hello? Who is this?!" Another female voice but much angrier. I knew that attitude anywhere. I sigh, "It's me, Katy. It's Jett."

The pause was so long I checked to make sure she didn't hang up on me. At this point, I would have expected it.

"Jett?! Where are you? Are you okay?" She's laughing and crying at the same time.

"I'm fine and safe, I promise."

"It's so good to hear your voice. I thought you were dead, but I never saw anything online. I searched for you every day."

"I left so I wouldn't be a burden to you and Mom. I was a screw-up and brought the family down. I thought it was best, especially with Dad on my neck. I couldn't take it anymore."

"Dad's dead, Jett."

It's like she snatched the oxygen from my lungs. Sure, I hated my dad for trying to turn me into him. I never thought I'd see the day when he was no longer on this Earth.

"I'm, I'm sorry. It was almost a year ago, he, he umm, had a heart attack at the mill after one of his drinking binges."

"I don't know what to say. Sorry, I wasn't there."

"I don't think it would have changed anything. He only became worse after you disappeared. All his anger for what you did went to all of us, but especially Dog. You'll be so proud that he pushed back. He instantly refused to follow Dad; he said he would run away too if Dad didn't back off and what that would do to his precious reputation."

I chuckled a bit, "That's my Dog. Tell him I'm so proud of him. I'm glad he knows he can be his own man."

"I can, and I am, Jett. I miss you." He chimes in, his voice so much deeper than the pipsqueak I was used to hearing. I now expect everyone to be standing or sitting around the phone. "I really am sorry to hear about Dad; no matter what I think, he was the love of Mom's life. I was calling because the group I'm with now has a woman who's like a mother to me, and she told me that no matter what happened, that mom would still love to hear from me."

"Jett, it's Chelsea. I'm so glad you're okay."

"I thought you all would be angry at me for leaving."

"Oh, Katy and I were! Until I read the letters, we all read each other's letters. It helped us understand why you did what you did. I wish you had talked to us, but I get it. We still miss you."

She left it at that. "I missed you all, too. It's so good to hear your voices after so long."

"Rocket, are you coming home?" Dog asked me. I almost forgot that hearing them call me by my nickname made me feel like their superhero.

"I'm not sure about that, Dog. I'm still a fugitive, and they'll lock me up the moment I cross city limits."

"You have to! Mama's sick!"

What I felt hearing about my dad was nothing compared to hearing those words. "What?" I squeaked out. It was like a shot to the gut and heart at the same time.

There was silence. "Somebody tell me! What's wrong with mama?"

"After you ran away, Mom and Dad had an intense fight. She screamed at him that he lost our boy. He said he would change all the locks and switch the home phone number, but she put her foot down and declared she would knock him over the head with a cast iron skillet if he changed the house number. She said that you'd call one day, and she'd be here to answer. She said, 'I know Jett will call, and it will be before it's too late.' That's when she told us about her stage two breast cancer diagnosis."

My heart sank. Cancer.

"Mama..."

So much guilt was tormenting me. Had I been there, would she have gotten sick? Would my presence make her fight harder so she wouldn't be so ill?

"Where is she?"

"Jett..."

"Goddammit, Katy, don't try to comfort me. It's my fault! I shouldn't have run away, or she wouldn't be fighting for her life."

"No, stop blaming yourself! She knows why you did it and prayed for your safety daily. We all do; there is not one ounce of ill will in this house. We only want you to be healthy and happy and know we will always love you."

They still love me, and it warms my heart that is hurting because my mother is sick.

"Thank you. I'm sorry, and I love you all more than anything. Can I talk to Mom? Is she there?"

"Of course, she's been listening since we all came into her room. You can say whatever you want to tell her. She had her treatment earlier today, so she's a bit weaker and lethargic."

I heard her clear her throat and exhaled; somehow I knew she wasn't doing good. I didn't even fight back the tears that fell.

"Mama? Mama, it's Jett."

"My sw-sweet baby Jett. I knew you would call before it was too late." She sounded so tired and winded.

"I love you, mama. I'm so sorry."

"Sorry? For what...I understand, and I hope...you're... happy."

"You sound so weak. How bad is it?"

"It's at the end stage now. Mama's decided to spend her final days at home. Doctors gave her only a few weeks, and that was two weeks ago."

There were so many emotions; the most present were anger and heartbreak. If I had not called, she could have been gone. And I'd never forgive myself.

"I...knew...you'd call. I needed to hear my sweet boy's

voice...before I died." Her labored breathing, trying to power through, but I could tell she was struggling hard.

"Mom, please don't say that. You're not going to die; you're a fighter, the strongest woman I know." I had to lean against the nearest tree; hearing her like that broke my heart.

"It's okay... I'm ready to be...with your father...again. You'll...take care of each other." Then she exhaled loudly.

I didn't want to think it.

"Mama! Mom!"

"It's okay; it took a lot of energy out of her. We're giving her a mild sedative so she can be in less pain. She's resting now. These bouts come and go."

I could only hear one sentence playing over and over in my head.

"Kat, Dog, Katy, Chelsea... I'll be home tomorrow."

They all started crying, but I could tell it was tears of joy—the black sheep was coming home.

I could tell they didn't want to let me off the phone for fear they'd never hear from me, so I spent another hour chatting about anything and everything. All the while, I was putting a to-do list in my head. Would I take my bike, or would I ask for the truck? If I ask for the truck, I'll have to explain

why. That part of my life is largely unknown to them; I've only told bits and pieces.

I take a few minutes after hanging up to pull myself together. I'm hoping Poppy was up and out of my room so I could pack my bag without interrogation.

I stroll back through the forest back into the yard. No one was outside, but I knew someone would be inside.

CHAPTER EIGHTEEN

HOOKED
THE MERCILESS FEW MC: DEVIL'S IGNITED
Briarswood, Mass.

I stepped in to see them huddled at the table. I thought maybe they were eating breakfast, which would be odd when we rarely eat together but in our preferred spots.

"There's the early riser. Where have you been?" Demon asked.

I held up the phone, "Had a call to make."

"Everything alright, son?" Lucifer is immediately in Papa Bear mode.

"We can talk later. Do we have club business?"

"Yeah, not 24 hours later, Sebastien notified me of a run to Brookside Treatment Facility. He said the shipment is docked, and they are currently loading the truck; he stated this is our audition to be his preferred club. We head down to the docks in an hour. Let's see how our test run goes."

That's code for if we don't get good vibes, he'll have to find someone else to do it.

"Grab breakfast and meet me outside at 11 am." I didn't even realize I had been outside for so long. That at least gives me some time to start packing. I won't need much.

I opened the door to see Poppy was gone. She hadn't brought any clothes, so she'd probably gone home to get changed. After hearing her brush with some perverted stranger in her room, I want to suggest she leave some things over here. Now that I know the bunny place wasn't safe, I would rather she stayed with me. If I see her, I know she's okay.

I grab my duffel bag and toss in a few shirts and jeans. I notice the bag with only a couple of pills left. I toss it in the bag. I figured I'd resign to asking for the truck, not wanting to bring attention to myself on my bike. I text Poppy and tell her she can leave some clothes in my room. She replied with a bunch of question marks and then a thumbs up.

I open my door to the wonderful smell of waffles. Sam and the girls have done it again with a spread fit for a King. I grab a couple of waffles, bacon, and an omelet. I sit at the bar, and Lila slides me an orange juice.

"Thanks, small fry."

She flips me off with a fake smile, "With all my love, *lapis pau bastardo.*" (Pencil dick bastard) She's been hanging around Avi too long, and now she chastises me in two languages. Whatever it was, it was vicious in the most Lila of ways. She resumes pouring glasses and handing them out.

By the time we finish breakfast, strap up, and warm up our bikes, it's a little after 11 am. Lucifer signals our departure by revving, and we follow two by two.

We get to the dock, and he's in a tailored suit and expensive sunglasses—quite the opposite of Frankie's bargain bin suits. Judging by the clothes, I'm sure those Italian loafers were authentic. He's easily wearing our runner's fee, if not more.

We parked side by side and dismounted. Sebastien opens his arms, "Welcome, Merciless Few. The shipment has been loaded onto the truck, and now I need you to get it there safely."

"Where is the manifesto?" It was the first statement out of the boss man's mouth. I saw Sebastien's face turn sour for a moment, and then he adjusted his cufflinks as a distraction before reaching for the clipboard inside the truck's cab. "Here you go, *el manifiesto* (the manifesto) with all the supplies listed. The gloves, masks, cold caps, syringes, it's all there."

Lucifer reads it while walking to the back. We follow and see him opening the door. "Reap, Fiend, check the load." I hop in first and start from the back, listing the supplies, including the ones he stated. Reap listed the ones in the front; we hopped back out and closed the doors once we cleared.

"See? *Completamente legitimo.* (Completely legit) I have no reason to lie to you. It's about trust." Lucifer doesn't respond; he hands the clipboard over to the driver.

"Everything's good. Mount up, boys, and make sure we're hot." That was the code for locked and loaded; there was no safety. We must be ready to pounce if he's as targeted as he says.

It was an easy load to secure and get to the cancer facility, and they looked so relieved to see the supplies. I look up and notice a couple of kids in the window, and it makes me sick. No one should have to face cancer, especially not children. They smile and wave when I see them, and I wave back. It's these types of deliveries that make it worth it. We helped offload and signed the manifesto. The driver confirmed delivery, and we headed home.

That delivery took up a chunk of time, and it was late afternoon by the time we got back. It was time I talked with Lucifer and Sam without tipping off the rest of the crew. I know Lucifer's habit of taking a shower when he got home from a job. I'd catch him before that. As usual, Sam greeted him, and they walked hand in hand toward their room. I followed quickly because I didn't want to interrupt anything. I hear Sam giggle before I knock. She opens the door. "Can I talk to you guys for a minute?" She agrees and opens the door. I didn't realize how big their quarters were; there was space for a seating area, and I sat on the couch. Sam sat on the bed, and Lucifer sat in a chair that mirrored his leather sofa in the living room.

"What is it, son?"

I think Sam could feel my hesitation, and she sat beside me. "I uh, I did what you said, Sam. I called her, and um... she's sick. She's dy-dying. I have to see her before it's too late. I wanted to ask to take the truck. I'd leave tonight to get there by the morning."

Lucifer looked so confused. Sam explains, "I told Jett that he should contact his family. I had a feeling to tell him that and I'm so glad I did. I'm so sorry, honey, that wasn't what I wanted you to find out. You take the truck and see her. Do you want someone to go with you?"

"No, I need to do this alone. I was going to tell you earlier when you asked, but we had this job to do."

Lucifer sighed. I could see he was unhappy that I had mixed up my priorities. "Son, that is more important than any job. You know we would never cut you out, but as Sam said, you need to go and see her. Don't waste any more time. Keep in touch, and we'll keep this to ourselves if you like?"

He knew the brothers would ask, but it's such a personal

issue that they didn't feel comfortable speaking about it without my permission.

"It's fine. They're my brothers. I know they will wonder, especially if I'm gone for a few days."

Sam touches my shoulder, "You take as long as you need. We'll be right here when you get back. Please send them our love."

"If you need an advance on your share, take it from the club funds."

"Nah, I think I'll be ok. Haverhill is even smaller than here." We all chuckle, and I sigh in relief. "Thank you, guys. I appreciate all you've done for me."

Sam smiles, "Well, dinner is ready for you heathens, so eat good for your drive back home, and I want updates on the road. I mean it!"

"Yes, ma'am." I feel relieved to finally tell someone. Since calling them, the thoughts have been rampant, and so has the self-abuse. Had I been there...

I had to focus on getting there. I appreciate my family here; they filled in when I needed them most, but now I must face my fears and go home.

CHAPTER NINETEEN

HOOKED
THE MERCILESS FEW MC: DEVIL'S IGNITED
Briarswood, Mass.

Before I grab something to eat, I immediately go to my room and pop another pill; this was out of stress, not pain or pleasure. At least I knew it would keep me alert through the night.

I stuffed the bag back in my duffel and began gathering my toiletries.

"Where are you going?" I jump when I see Poppy lying down in my bed. She sat up, her hair deliciously tousled. She was again wearing one of my shirts, this time off the shoulder. I could see the bottom of her shorts. "What are you doing in here?"

"You said I could put some of my clothes in here. I put away some things and got sleepy; I thought I'd nap until you guys returned from your job. Don't ignore the question, where are you going?"

"I'm going home."

"That's great! I always feel like it's a sensitive subject, but hopefully, after we visit, it won't be..."

"We?"

"Yes, I'm going with you."

"Absolutely not. I do this alone."

"You're leaving at night, popped a pill, and expect to drive through the night safely? It would help if you had a second driver, and that's me. This time, I won't take no for an answer." She stood on business as she strolled past me and bent over to reach the bottom drawer. She grabbed a few pairs of shorts, underwear, and bras.

"How much did you bring from the bunny house?" She smirks while opening my t-shirt drawer and grabbing a few of mine. "Enough. Now, when do we leave?" She stood with her hand on her hip, looking up at me, daring to say she couldn't go. I relent, "After dinner. Come on. And no one knows but Sam and Lucifer; they'll tell everyone else later."

She stands on her tiptoes, zipping her lip, "Yes, sir." If I didn't need to focus on the drive ahead, I'd fuck that smart-ass mouth of hers, but another time. I grab her waist and pull her against me, "You're becoming a spoiled brat, you know that?"

"You're the one allowing it to happen." She smiles and turns to walk away. "You like it."

During dinner, I decided we would wait for everyone to turn in because I didn't want to answer any questions. Sam even announced that there would be no activities tonight and that we had worked hard today. Her being the club mom, no one would dare cross her. They'd have to go to Throttle for the night if they wanted to party.

We stayed in my room after dinner. It was around 10 pm when I took a peek, and the house was dark. Poppy was dropping a few more things in my bag when I signaled it was time to go.   I grabbed the keys on the way out. I see Wicked and Demon's bikes are gone; they went to Throttle for some fun. Reaper most likely went home, and Lucifer was in his room. I could see the light from under his door. I wanted to leave before I heard anything.

I signal her to follow me, and she turns off my light. I open the truck door for her, and she slides a blanket over the seat before placing the bag on the floor. She had taken one of my pillows, which she had set on her lap. I hop in and slam the door, causing her to jump; I chuckle. "Not funny. I thought we were being discreet?" She whisper yelled.

"Everyone who doesn't know is gone. We're good to go. Are you ready? Did you let anyone know at the bunny house?"

"Nah, they think I'm probably with you for the night, which technically, they are right." She squeezes my hand to get me to look at her, "Thank you for letting me ride along. I know you didn't want me to go."

It's not that I didn't want her to go; it's a complicated situation now that I know my dad is dead and my mom is on her deathbed. I know I wouldn't be able to handle this alone. Her softness and understanding as a woman made her the best choice to keep me sane.

An hour in, she was cuddled against me with the pillow between us. I turn the radio to something to pass the time. It took four hours to cross state lines; by then, I could feel the pill start to wear off, and I started yawning. I shook my head, causing Poppy to wake up. She pressed her hands against me and pushed to stretch her arms. "Where are we? What time is it?"

"Umm, crossed the state line into Vermont. It's about three or four hours to Haverhill. It's almost 3 a.m."

"You're yawning. It's time for you to switch. I put the town into my GPS. I should be good. Pull over at that gas station. We'll fill up and switch. No arguments."

I needed to rest my eyes in the worst way. I pull in and line the gas tank up. I go in to pay, and she's pumping the gas when I come out.

I stretch while walking, "That's my job."

"Don't even try to pull that chauvinistic bullshit. Equal opportunity, remember?" Reminding me of our conversation on the day of the charity ride. I hold my hands up and take my place on the passenger side. She finishes up and hops into the driver's seat. "Ready to be the passenger princess?" My eyes bucked; I never used that phrase, and now I know why. It's horrible. She winked, but I didn't answer. She starts it up, and we're on the familiar roads back home.

I don't know when I fell asleep, but I woke up to her holding my hand and rubbing her thumb across it. I sat up, and she smiled, "Hey, we're almost there. Is there a hotel we can crash at for a few hours? You want to be fresh when you see them because you look terrible." I blindly fix my hair before looking around to see we are indeed very close, about 20 minutes away. I'm trying to jog my memory, "Yeah, there's a small hotel named Sunshine Inn we can go to."

"Okay, I'll put it in the GPS. Do you feel better after your nap?"

"Yeah, you need me to take over?"

"No, I'm good. I can sleep at the hotel while you go see your family."

I was confused. I thought she was taking this opportunity to see a little piece of myself. "I thought you wanted to see my family or know why I'm here?"

"I mean, I do, but I'm not exactly the type men take to meet their family. Nobody wants to see their son with a whore." I saw her flinch as the word left her lips.

"You're not a whore. None of you are. You are dedicated to the club; what you do and how you enjoy life is nobody's business. I want you to meet my family."

"Really?" She squeaked out. "Yes, really." She sat up a little straighter, knowing she would meet them.

We finally found our way to the small hotel near the outskirts of town. Signing in as Mr. and Mrs. Smith gave Poppy a laugh. "Guess this is as close as I'm going to get, huh? I'm hopping in the shower first."

When she does, I call and leave a message that I was here and that I'll be by in an hour with a friend. I sit at the edge of the bed because I will have to explain everything to Poppy. I rub my hands and somehow feel comfort in that gesture. She comes out with a towel on her head and only that towel. As my eyes ventured down, I felt myself wanting to pin her against the wall, the bed...

"There are only two bath towels, and since you've seen me naked..." She shrugs, grabbing a bra and panty from the bag, then one of my shirts, which swallows her up. She notices I haven't moved. "Hey, are you showering?"

"Poppy, I need to tell you why I'm here. It's...it's serious." I kept my tone flat, and she looked concerned. She put on her clothes, including modest shorts, which just about covered everything. Then she sat beside me, crossed her legs, and took my hand.

"I promise anything you tell me will stay with me." I felt my throat tighten as I swallowed hard, taking the deepest breath of my life. "I found out my mom is dying of cancer, and my dad is already dead in the same call. There are so many emotions. I feel guilty and angry; if I hadn't run away, would she have gotten sick? Was I the last straw that caused my dad to drink himself to death? Did I cause this chain of events?"

"What?! No, how could you think that? The events that have happened were already written. You had nothing to do with that. I'm so sorry about your dad. You couldn't prevent that, but you can give your mom some relief to know that her son is alive and doing okay for himself. I know she misses you dearly, so shower and get ready. No matter what happens, you make this day the best for the woman

who gave you life and loves you unconditionally. You can do this, Fiend."

"Jett, or Rocket as my brother and sister call me."

She smiled so wide, "That's utterly adorable. Come on, let's not waste more time." She's right. I shower quickly and throw on a plain black shirt and blue jeans. It feels weird not to wear my cut.

My stomach drops when I pull up to the house, and I can see my hands shaking. I felt this emptiness knowing that my father wasn't there and that he was buried in Crestwood Memorial Cemetery, where our family has a huge plot of land.

Poppy was fidgeting with her hair and checking herself out in the mirror. She did a low ponytail that was braided and hardly any makeup. It was a fresh-faced type of beauty. We're both terrified of what they'll think. I make the first move and step out, and she follows. I reach for her hand when we meet in front of the truck. I look down, and she squeezes my hand in comfort. I take the first step forward and soon we're on the porch. Poppy held the flowers I bought for Mom, and I saw her legs shaking.

I knocked, and we waited; it was super early, but I'd lose my mind at the hotel. I needed to see my mom, and she needed to see me.

I heard running, definitely from the second floor. "He's

here! He's here!" Then the door rips open, and I'm face to face with Dog, who tackles me hard. I can barely stay up. "OOF! Hey, not so little brother." His arms tighten, and I realize he's crying. I separate his hands, and he stands up straight. "Hey, it's okay. I'm here; where is everyone?" He wipes his tears away, slightly embarrassed, when he sees Poppy beside me. "Kat's coming. Katy and Chelsea are making a big breakfast. Come in, come in!" He pulls me in with the strength of three grown men. He looked like a stockier version of Dad.

Poppy's looking around, taking in the family pictures. There are so many dorky pictures of me. I hope she meant what she said about the details of this visit staying with her.

"Douglas, this is my friend Poppy. Poppy, my little brother Doug, who we call Dog."

She held out her hand, and he shook it, "It's nice to meet you."

"Rocket!" Kat screams from the top of the stairs as she runs down them to get to me. I brace for the hit. She is a beautiful young lady in her prim and proper summer dress with sunflowers, a carbon copy of Mom. She steps back after hugging me, smiling at Poppy. "Poppy, this is Katarina, or Kat, my baby sister."

Poppy's eyes widened when she realized, "Oh my gosh, Kat and Dog, that is so cute!" They exchange pleasantries and then pull us into the kitchen.

There, my sisters had cooked up a storm. Katy was the brains of the operation, pointing and telling Chelsea what to do next. Katy turned around when she heard the commotion of them dragging us in. She nudged Chelsea violently, and she almost dropped the plate of biscuits. "Oh my god, Rocket! You're here, you're really here!" They both hugged me, and it was at that moment that I knew my trip was worth it. My sisters had aged, but it hadn't shown in their bright smiles.

Only Katy had a considerable amount of gray showing. Probably the stress of taking care of mom and family. Both their eyes shift away from me. "Oh, sorry. Katy, Chelsea, this is my friend Poppy. Poppy, my big sisters."

"So nice to meet you." I think their smiles got even wider. Oh, brother.

"Sit! We just finished breakfast. Mama is still resting, and I'll wake her in 30 minutes, enough time for you to fill up. How long was your drive, and where were you coming from?"

I never said I would only be a state away in my letters. "More than eight hours, but we split the driving. I'm in Massachusetts now."

"Typical Rocket, not sharing the details. Are you ashamed of us?" Katy says jokingly, but the situation makes me think. Is that what it was? Did I make it sound like I was ashamed of them?

Katy chucks a dish towel at me, "Stop it, Rocket. You always overthink. I was joking. We know why you left. You gave us closure, not to worry ourselves, and to know that you were making your life better. And I see you have, and I know Poppy's keeping you in line."

Poppy nodded; she was confident, knowing they weren't judging her. She dug into her plate. "Oh my goodness, everything is so good and homemade. I wish I knew how to cook like this."

"You'll need to keep my little brother fed. Does he still eat like a horse?" I looked down at my plate; it was full, but it looked normal to me. Do I eat like a horse? "Yes, he does, but all the guys do, and that's why we make these buffet-style meals. That's how I'm slowly learning how to cook."

I could see that they had many questions. "I...am part of a motorcycle club, and we all live together in a clubhouse."

Dog's eyes lit up, "Cool! A biker gang!" I hold my hand up,

"It's not like what you read or see on TV; it's not SOA. We protect women and children from those who harm them."

He's still grinning, "That's still so cool. Can I be in the group when I get a bike?" I never knew he was interested in bikes, but I left when he was a kid, and now he is a teenager. He'd need a custom-sized one. He's about five or six inches taller than me and still growing.

"You keep your grades up, graduate, then we'll talk. Mom would want you to make something of yourself, not be like me." Poppy poked me, "Hey, don't do that. You are a great person and role model."

"She's right, Rocket. You chose your path; I have always told them they could do the same since you left. They were meant to live their own lives, their dreams. Why didn't you come back on your bike?"

"I'm still a fugitive; I didn't want to cause a scene." Chelsea scoffed, "All those old, ignorant, incompetent men are dead. The new Captain threw out your warrant along with any other suspicious ones. You can come home anytime you want."

I sighed in relief; I was no longer a criminal or fugitive.

"Hey, why don't you go wake mom up. I know it would make her day."

I look away, trying not to tear up; I know she wouldn't look the same, but how bad would it be? She's in the end stage of her fight; would I even recognize her? Poppy squeezed my hand, placing the flowers near me. "Remember what I said."

I stare at her and then kiss her forehead. I stand and take the flowers. Katy and Chelsea lead me upstairs and stop at the door. "No matter what you see, remember Mom how she was before you left." That was going to be hard because she was a tired, fed-up woman who turned to drugs for relief.

Like her son.

I acknowledge, and when she opens the door, I hear the

beeps and clicks of machines. The room was dark, but they could navigate easily, doing this every day. I stayed where I was until Katy slowly opened the blinds, and I could see the woman who owned my heart. I broke down, slapping my hand over my mouth. She was thinner, smaller, weaker. I noticed how loose her wedding ring was on her delicate finger. Her once dark hair was gray but that beautifully grayed like Katy was getting. She inhaled quickly, and her eyes slowly opened.

"Good morning, mom. Someone's here to see you." Chelsea could barely contain her tears as she pointed at me. Mom slowly turned her head, and finally, I could lay eyes on my mother.

"My, my baby Jett." She slowly held her hand out, and I never moved so fast to sit and take her hand. I wiped her tears while allowing mine to fall; they were cathartic. "Mom, I'm so sorry that I left you! You didn't deserve to worry; you didn't deserve this. I should have been here!" I know everyone understood, but I couldn't understand how my mom went from being a perfect housewife and mom to fighting for her life. I cried against her hand, kissing it incessantly. My mother, my lovely mother, was withering away.

"Stop crying, my love." She looked behind me and smiled, "You brought me my favorite flowers." She was winded but not as bad as when I first heard her. Chelsea raised her bed a bit so Mom could sit up comfortably. I hand her the flowers; she slowly brings them to her nose and inhales the sunflowers and roses. "Mmm, they smell divine. Katy, can you put these in a vase for me?" She started to sound normal. "Sure, mama. We'll bring up breakfast so you guys can talk."

I find myself trying to burn infinite images of my mom in my brain to make up for lost time. "You look so handsome, like your father." She paused, and I saw her swallow hard. "I'm sure you know..."

"Yes, mama, I'm so sorry."

"Please stop saying sorry; none of this is your fault. Not one day. The only thing I want, other than

seeing you, is to know you all will have each other once I'm gone."

"Mom, please."

"Hush, I've made my peace. I don't want you to mourn me. I want you to celebrate the good times. To stay connected and take care of each other. Do you hear me, Jett Avery Watkins?" I could only laugh. There was the mom I knew, her voice filled with a mix of determination and love.

"Yes, mama."

"Good. Now tell me everything."

I spent the next few minutes telling her my life in the Cliffs note version. I even told her about the incarceration; I knew she wouldn't judge me. She tells me it's a life lesson and a part of me.

"Tell me, are you seeing someone, or perhaps I already have a grandbaby?" She gave me a sweet smile as I almost choked; I shouldn't have been surprised, but now that she knew my life, what made her think I'd be a family man?

I chuckle, and she pats my hand, "A woman can dream, can't she?" Then the door opened, and Katy had a cup in her hand, but behind her was Poppy. She had tried to make herself even more modest than earlier. Poppy was meeting my mother. My mom's eyes grew big, and she smiled, putting her hand on her face, "Oh, I must look a mess. Who is this beautiful girl?"

Poppy blushes as she steps forward. "Hi, I'm Poppy. Jett and I are friends." She places her hand on my shoulder. Mom looks at me and smiles. I know that smile; it's universal mom language.

"It is wonderful to meet you, Poppy. I hope the looks of a

sick woman don't frighten you." Poppy nudges me, and I move so she can sit down; she grabs my mom's hand. "Never apologize. You are a fighter and so beautiful; it radiates like the sun. I can see where the girls get their looks. I am honored to have met you, and since finding out, I have been praying for your strength and health. He needs his mother."

I could have never expected this. They were immediately bonded in a way I would never understand. Mom shakes her head as Katy hands her the cup. "He only needed to lay eyes on me. And I'm so glad he did; I can rest in peace." It sounded so morbid, and I know she said she was ready to die, but I wasn't prepared to let her go. I just got her back.

She sips from the cup and smiles at my sisters, "Thank you. I can barely taste the meds this time." She sets down the cup on the tray next to her. Then she shifts toward Poppy. "Tell me, Poppy, does my son make you happy?"

"What?"

"A mother's intuition is powerful, and I can sense it. Regardless of your label on this relationship, I want to know whether he fills your heart with joy?" Poppy's eyes meet mine, not searching for an answer but to gauge my reaction. She turns back, her voice steady, "Yes, he brings me happiness."

I knew she meant it. My mom's smile is even bigger, "Then that's all that matters." My mom seemed to get her energy from our conversation; she didn't seem sick by the night's end. I stepped away for a few minutes to let Sam and Lucifer know we were okay. I came back to see Poppy taking a selfie with everyone. She fit in perfectly even though she felt they would judge her. It had never been the case; in fact, they squeezed her dry for embarrassing stories about me. She kept her stories PG, but they soaked up every word.

We gathered for dinner in the coziness of her room; the scent of freshly made sandwiches and chips filled the air.

Mom, her strength waning, sat up in bed with Chelsea in the recliner and Katy perched on the bed corner. Poppy, always considerate, had taken the chair, and I found my place on the other corner of the bed. Then, my mom, a figure of strength and love, looked around and cried, "It's so good to see all of you together. It's what I prayed for, more than healing myself because I know you'll always be there for each other." My siblings and I nodded. Our hearts heavy with unspoken understanding.

My mom pointed to Kat, "Kat, bring me the last copy of mine and your father's will for Jett." Kat turns around and opens the cabinet, grabbing a stack of papers rolled up with a rubber band. She gets up and hands it to me. I pull off the rubber band and unroll it and a debit card falls out. I held onto the card and skimmed the paperwork to see that she had a million-dollar policy to which we were all to split when she died.

"Your father had the same policy, and I put your share in an account; that's the card. The pin is your birthday. When I die, you'll get the same amount deposited."

I couldn't take hearing it anymore. "Please stop saying you're going to die. You haven't even acted like you're sick. Maybe...maybe you're getting better!" I could see the tears in my sibling's eyes, indicating they knew something I didn't.

"Sit down, Jett." Poppy stood up, "Should I go?"

"No, dear, you need to hear to help my son. Son, have you never heard of people looking like they were getting better only for them to pass away not too long after? This is what this is..."

No! I refuse to believe her! The angry tears rolled down my face, and she squeezed my hands to force me to look at her. "I told them that once I saw you, I could let go. To not worry about my baby being out there in the streets or worse. I prayed and said I would be happy to go home if I knew you were okay. To meet your dad at the gates and spend an eternity in love. To reunite with the ones I've already lost and to wait for you all."

I shake my head. I wouldn't accept it, "No, mama, no! I just got you back. I need you! I love you, don't leave me!" I was distraught and heartbroken because I knew she meant it and that it would happen. Happen on her terms and that's what she wanted. She let me cry and process everything she said, and eventually, I knew I had to be okay with her wishes, her dying wishes.

"I'll never leave you, Rocket. I'll be with you always, with all of you, and I am confident that Poppy will keep you on the right path."

"Yes, ma'am, I will." She said as she continued to rub my back.

"Don't hurt her. Her heart is special, and it's only for you." I could only nod. She continues to look at all the people surrounding her. "This is exactly what I wanted."

An hour later, we were at the front door. "Are you sure you don't want to stay here? Even though Dog took your old room, we can temporarily put him back in the room with Kat."

"No, he finally earned the right to have his own space; besides, our clothes are there. I'll be back in the morning." I embrace each family member, feeling their warmth and love, and Poppy follows, a loyal companion on this journey.

"Thanks for letting me in your home. Everyone made me feel so comfortable."

"You take care of our Rocket. You heard what our Mama said." She waved to them as she returned to the truck, leaving me with them.

"We love you, Jett."

"And I love you guys. Give Mama another kiss good night for me." I hug everyone, kiss my sister's forehead, and reach for my keys as I leave the house. My heart is heavy with a whirl-wind of emotions, a storm of anger threatening to consume me. It's all too much, too fast, and I feel a numbness creeping in.

I step in, and she's looking away, I assume very deep in thought, so we drove back in silence.

CHAPTER TWENTY

HOOKED
THE MERCILESS FEW MC: DEVIL'S IGNITED
Briarswood, Mass.

Poppy sits on the bed and exhales loudly, looking at me. She wants to say something, and I'm sure I
   don't want to hear it. She's rubbing her hands together, and then she stops. It's not good.
   "She's going to die."
   "I know that!" I yell, feeling the emotional wall crumbling.
   "What are you going to do? How are you going to cope?" I didn't fucking know. How do you expect someone to deal with actively losing a parent, especially when I have already lost one? I was so angry, angry I couldn't fix it.
   I exploded, "How am I going to deal? By numbing myself, that's how! No one wants to deal with shit like this! As if my life isn't crap enough, now I have to accept that my mother...is

dying...of cancer?!" I grab the pills and see the instant disappointment in her eyes. "As far as the next few hours go, none of my problems exist, and I don't want to hear about it."

"Jett..." I didn't want to talk about it anymore. "Fiend," I said viciously, to hurt her so she'd stop probing and finally shut up. Her eyes welled up immediately, and she looked away as I popped the pill, eager to feel nothing.

"Whatever." She moves to the other twin bed, takes off her shoes and shorts, and slides between the

sheets. I stood there, surprised. Briefly seeing her pink butterfly underwear got me riled up.

"You don't want to take advantage of my high and horny state?" I chuckle, and she looks over her shoulder at me in disgust.

"Sure, when you are looking for a marathon fuck, not when you're trying to fuck away your feelings because you don't want to face the fact that the number one woman in your life might not live for much longer. Would you want her to see you like this right now?" She lay back down, covering her entire body with the blanket.

I could only stand there.

Then the anger surged, "Maybe after this shower, I'll go to the bar and find someone else to take care of me, huh, maybe even two! Every girl loves a badass biker boy." She didn't stir. She was silently calling my bluff, daring me to do some stupid shit, and having the unyielding audacity to bring it back to this room.

I resign myself to the shower and spend a good deal letting the water pound my back. My senses heightened, so it felt heavenly everywhere. I hold my hand over my scar and enjoy the massage-like treatment of the shower. I dry off with a fresh towel, and it looks like they cleaned the place. I wrapped it around my waist and walked out into the air conditioner, blasting. I quickly put on clothes and observed her still sleeping.

I was wide awake. She was right; I would never fuck someone in my hometown let alone bring them here. But what was I supposed to do? Poppy shifted and I remember how my mom's eyes lit up when she would glance at us. My mind was so muddied with so much I couldn't sit here. I grab my key card and slip out.

The route to Haverhill was one of those roads you didn't fear being on in the middle of the night. I headed toward town. I kept walking and thinking, enjoying the joys of the highlights of today and letting out muffled screams of my frustration. I also thought about my brothers and Sam; they have always been my strength and sanity.

I realized I had been walking for an hour straight, covered a lot of ground, and had zero solutions. This isn't a resolving type of walk but a way to vent my emotions. I stop, which causes me to yawn and stretch instinctively. I started to regret walking this far knowing I had to walk back.

Shit!

When I turn around, I'm blinded by high-beam lights headed my way. I hear it accelerate before the brakes squealing right in front of me. Someone jumps out and leaves the door open; it's Poppy.

She hugs me, then shoves me hard, "What the hell were you thinking?! It's half past fucking midnight. I woke up, and you were gone! I... I..." She was so pissed she stopped to inhale and exhale, running her hands through her hair; then her lip started to quiver, which further angered her.

I didn't mean to scare her. I grab her, but she pushes me and does every time I try until I wrap my arms around her. "I thought you were going out to find someone else to fuck?" She sneered at me.

"You know I wouldn't. I needed to get out; the room was closing in on me with all the thoughts running through my head and I panicked. I don't know what to do, Poppy. I don't know what to do."

I was vulnerable as I held on to her like she was the last person on Earth. We're on the shoulder with the truck still in the road, and she's rubbing her hands up and down my back, comforting me. I feel peace in her arms. She separates us and looks up at me. There's so much sexual tension, so many emotions, it's all building up. Her arms are around my neck, and my hands are on her face. My resolve snapped, and I devoured her lips and hoisted her on my waist. She whimpers as if she hadn't been touched in months. I break free to drive us back to the room.

A few hours later, I was staring at the smooth skin of her back, the rest of her naked body covered by the blanket. I turned on the TV with the volume on low; I couldn't go back to sleep. I shifted to my back, sliding the sheet down to my waist. The AC felt so good on my still sweat-covered skin. I turned to a movie I didn't need the volume for, I knew it word for word. Poppy turns over and looks at me. She stretches, causing the blanket to slide down to her waist, teasing me with those piercings I had in between my teeth earlier. I sat up, and she plopped her pillow on my lap and laid across it. I play in her hair, "Morning. It's still pretty early, so you can go back to sleep."

"Why don't you?"

"As much as you tried to wear me out, I still have a ton on my mind. Not like I haven't had insomnia before."

"That doesn't make it ok, especially with you riding a motorcycle. It's dangerous, and I'm worried, Fiend." I kissed her temple "Jett." She smiled, and then I pulled her up to me, and we got a couple more hours of rest.

We spent the whole day and night with mom and family. Mom told me my mission was complete and that I should head home. Katy and Chelsea had the instructions on what to do when the time came. Instead of fighting and arguing, I agreed, and she kissed my cheek, telling me how proud she was.

"Mom, I can stay another day, another few days! I can do my laundry at the house. They said I could take as much time as I need."

"No, your family needs you. We have all your contact info, and I'm sure Dog and Kat will be calling you so much, but your place is in Massachusetts with her. Don't fight the attraction; you're trying so hard, and it's so obvious. You may not give me grandbabies, but you can give me peace by making sure you have someone. She's your peace, Jett."

I look over, and the girls are talking to Kat about makeup and spilling their best-kept secrets. She thrives in all this female attention. I tune in, "Yeah, Kat has a boyfriend at school. His name is Denver." All the girls ooh, and I stand up, "Boyfriend? Where does this boy live? I want to meet him." I growl. Apparently, Mom gave her the all-clear to start dating, but I'm immediately in big brother mode. Kat rolls her eyes, "Dog already threatened to knock his teeth down his throat if he hurts me. Don't worry; he's done great at being overprotective while you've been gone."

"He's some dorky nerd. Zero threat, bro." Dog exclaims before laughing. Then, Kat chucks a book at his head. "Shut up!" Dog ducks in time.

Mom shifts in her bed and winces. "Katy, it's time for my dose. Chelsea, my anti-nausea pill, please. I want to get ahead of it this time." Katy has the syringe ready to inject into her IV line but waits until Mom swallows the huge pill in her hand. It looks too big. "Don't worry, I've been getting these down for a while now. I want you to call me when you get home and make sure Poppy's around sometime so I can say hi."

I keep quiet about her practically staying with me. Poppy doesn't hesitate to kiss Mom on her forehead and whisper in her ear. My mom's smile is so beautiful. It's that moment in time I'll hold in my heart forever. "Thank you. Take care of yourself, dear."

It was my turn. I hesitate, prolonging it as much as I can. "Say goodbye, Jett. Your heart is here, but your home...is with them. I regret I never met them, but I know they take good care of you. That's all I could ever want. I love you so much, Chipmunk. I'm so proud of you, of all of you." Her tired eyes filled with tears. I could tell by her wheezing that she needed to rest. "Now go before I take my dose. I don't want you to see me like that. Remember the good times, which is every day that we were all together." I bend down and hug her, but not too tight in her frail state. I feel her chuckle against me and step back to see that bright smile that makes me smile.

"That's my boy." I wait downstairs for everyone with Poppy. She hugged me as she sat in my lap. Katy closes the door softly and makes her way downstairs. I tapped Poppy on her leg, and she stood up, then I did. It was an awkward silence until Kat hugged me hard, and then Dog hugged me on the other side, causing some pain. Chelsea followed, and finally, Katy covered me in loving warmth. There were no tears this time; we were all at peace. I heard a click and saw Poppy had taken a photo.

"Keep me updated, especially when...you know, it happens."

Katy reaches back and grabs the family photo we took after church one day. I kicked and screamed, but Mom convinced me to be still for once in my life, and this was the result. I hold it and chuckle; I'm glad I did.

"We will. Just so you know, we decided that after everything is settled with their estates, we're going

to sell the house, it's time for us to think about the future, especially when these two leave the nest."

"Rocket, can I come visit you one day?"

"Yeah, me too. I want to meet your biker friends."

I kiss them both on the forehead. "We'll see; perhaps we can arrange a road trip for you all to come down there. Only if you stay out of trouble, okay?" They nod eagerly.

I give them a wave before heading back to the hotel. We packed up, and I let Sam know we were on our way back.

We pulled up to the house slightly after sunrise, and I noticed all the bikes lined up outside the front door. They must have had another run. It was confirmed when I saw them all passed out in the living room—it sounded like a cave full of bears. I see movement and know that it's Sam. We quietly made our way to the kitchen. Sam looked so relieved to see us. "Oh my gosh, I'm so glad you are back! Poppy, I didn't know you went, but I'm glad you did."

Sam looks over and holds her arms out, and I hug her; the hug is filled with solace. "How is she?"

"Not good; she believes now that she's seen me that she'll go any day now. I have to be okay with that, but the time I spent was more than I could have ever expected. They still love me."

Sam punches my arm, "Of course they do! Don't be stupid; your quick decision doesn't diminish their love for you. They understood and welcomed you back with open arms. I'm glad you're back; maybe I'll get to speak to her on the phone one day?"

"Sure."

"Okay, go rest or change. Breakfast is at 8 a.m. Poppy, do you need me to drop you off at the bunny house?"

"No, I got some of my things here in his room; I'm okay, Miss Sam, thank you." The smile that radiated from Sam could light the whole house. I leave before she corners me for answers.

I didn't have any, but everything Sam and Mom said had been replaying in my head about Poppy. It did not fall on deaf ears, but I pretended not to hear.

I'm so exhausted, having driven the whole time, I plop down on my bed and exhale. Then my bed dips and I feel weight on my back. I look back to see Poppy's legs as she straddles me.

"I don't have the energy, Pops. Not even a pill could revive me."

"Take off your shirt, you horny perv. I'm giving you a massage." I slipped it off, and her hands immediately slid from the small part of my back to my shoulders. Her hands are like fucking magic, and I groan as she works my tight and tired muscles. She even used her forearms to get deeper, "Goddammit Poppy, you are an angel, an angel with a whore's mouth." She laughs out loud, "Thanks, I think? Now shut up and rest." She worked me for another 20 minutes, and then it was time for breakfast.

CHAPTER TWENTY-ONE

HOOKED
THE MERCILESS FEW MC: DEVIL'S IGNITED
Briarswood, Mass.

The days ahead were filled with Kat and Dog calling me every day, multiple times a day. I was okay with that. They were making up for lost time. I admit that every time Katy or Chelsea spoke, my heart would sink. I wondered if this was the day they said that Mama was gone. It had only been a week since I had been home, but the stress of not knowing caused some familiar irritation and intrusive thoughts.

Good, not great...

Poppy did her best to keep me occupied with small outings and meaningless tasks like the weekly grocery run—any opportunity to spend time together. And I appreciated her trying to keep my mind off of needing the pills. I still thought about them, especially when I was down to the final three.

Do you know those days or weeks when everything is off or goes wrong? I was super irritated at what had taken place these past few days. First, since I had not taken a pill in a while, I recognized my irritation as detox. My moods were unstable, and everything and everyone tested my patience. I was trying my damndest not to explode. Then my Destiny's throttle started to act up, and that's no one-step problem. I had Reaper check the carburetor and engine. Those were areas I was not familiar with or comfortable tearing apart. He gave me the all-clear, which was good. I did not have the funds to replace it or, in turn, get a new bike. He suggested I check the air and fuel filters and the spark plugs. These are more manageable tasks but still pretty time-consuming. I spent the time complaining to myself about the constant pain of bending down. Finally, I figured out my fuel filter and plugs needed replacing, which cost me a bit but not as much as a major component. I grabbed the keys to the truck, and Poppy jumped up. "Not today, Poppy!" I yell, then storm out. When I returned, I slammed the truck door harder than usual. I go to fix Destiny and do not have to deal with the consequences of my actions.

Three hours later, she was running like new, finally a break in this spiral. I sighed in relief.

Ring ring

I stood to pull my phone from my pocket and saw the familiar number, and without warning, my stomach dropped. I fell to my knees before even answering. It went beyond the five standard rings because they needed me to answer.

I knew.

I knew.

The lump slammed my throat as I tried to choke it down. I hit answer, and there was silence, then sniffling; she was trying not to cry over the phone, but my tears had already started.

"P-Please no..." I choked out.

"I'm so sorry, Rocket. Mama's...mama's gone..." Then she let the emotion overwhelm her and sobbed over the phone.

I should have been there. I should have gone back; maybe I should have never left. I left her there to die!

I left her!

"I'm coming home," I state with no room for misunderstanding.

"No, wait. She left a message for me to read to you; she said: My dearest son, I know your first emotion will be sadness followed by guilt. You have nothing to feel guilty for. You fulfilled my dying wish to see you; this overwhelming calm washed over me when I did. It was peace. I ask one thing in my death: that you do not come back. Your home is there. Your sisters will relocate to begin their lives after taking such good care of me. I encouraged it. I love you, Jett. You were always enough for me. Now, be enough for yourself and anyone who may enter your life. Love, Mom."

I was so lost that I couldn't speak, and I think Chelsea knew. "Jett, you have to grant Mama's wish. Once we've settled, I'll give you all the information."

My brain was blurry, filled with static, and not comprehending. All I knew was my mother was dead. My first love, the woman who raised me, was my light in this dark world, and now that light is gone.

I can't deal with this. I need to go.

"I can't do this!" I yell, then hang up my phone. The tears blind my vision as I kneel to the ground in a ball.

I don't want to feel like this.

I don't want to feel, and I knew what to do.

I tried to gather myself, but I was trying not to sob openly. I needed to get to the safety of my room, my sanctuary.

I wipe the tears, take a deep breath to stop my lips from

quivering, and walk normally into the house. I saw Avi playing with Raven while Reaper was tending to their son, Onyx, and I felt white-hot anger and overwhelming sadness thinking about the time I lost with my mother after I ran away.

It wasn't enough time!

I close the front door, and they acknowledge me; I keep silent to avoid the soul-crushing pain. I see the bunnies in their gossip circle and beeline it to my room and my stash. My foggy brain makes me confused about where I put them. I move them every so often to avoid Poppy finding them again.

I was getting frustrated, and that allowed the tears to fall, but they were of anger that I couldn't find them. I tossed my room, "Hey, what are you doing?" Poppy says as she closes the door. I found my gym bag. "Not now." They weren't there, so I checked the nightstand drawer where I once hid them, then my gym shoes, and finally, between my bed and my pillow, and there they were. I stood up and sighed in relief when I saw two pills left.

"Wait! You don't need to take those. You were getting better."

"I thought you said they made me perform better?! You should be excited; you will benefit from this!" I spat maliciously.

"Not when it makes you like this. This isn't the Jett I know. Why are you taking them? What's wrong? Tell me."

"Stop calling me Jett!" I screamed. "I never gave you permission to call me anything other than Fiend."

"But you did." She squeaked, trying to figure out if she was afraid or mad. At this point, I couldn't care less.

"Fiend is who I am, and you're just a bunny, a notch in my fucking belt, nothing more." She flinched hard, and I wiped the tears away angrily, then popped the last two pills while she shook her head.

Her face softened; she wasn't giving up, "You don't mean that. You let me stay with you because you were worried about me. I met your family...your mother." Her eyes filled with tears, but she fought tooth and nail not to let them fall. She was angry I was being so vicious; she wanted to help, but I wanted to hurt. Then she slapped her hand over her mouth. She hugged me instantly but didn't say anything. She looks up and places her hand on my cheeks. I'm struggling; I can feel it coming to a head, and I hate it.

"Baby, I'm so sorry. It's okay." She tried to comfort me, but I didn't want to accept it. I shoved her off me, "What do you know, huh?!"

She looked enraged. "She's dead! Your mother is dead, and you chose to numb your feelings again instead of expressing them like a normal fucking adult. It's okay to cry! She was a beautiful soul, but you knew this was coming. She wouldn't want to see you like this, hopped up on drugs!" She was getting too loud for my comfort.

"You need help, Jett. Help from your brothers. Let them..." She was reaching for the door.

I snapped and grabbed her by her throat, slamming her against the door, "If you tell anyone, I'll..." I didn't finish as Lucifer, and my brothers violently opened the door.

It distracted me until Poppy swung her fist and connected with my jaw. "Do what you want, you fucking asshole! You can rot in hell for all I care! She would be SO disappointed in you! You don't have to worry about me bothering you anymore! I'm

done!" She grabs her bag and what is visible and storms past everyone. The girls follow.

I rubbed my jaw.

"What the hell has gotten into you?" I heard Sam before I saw her. I wanted to be left alone. She squared up to me, daring me to say something the least bit disrespectful. "Nothing. She needed to know her place, and it's NOT with me." I sat on my bed and looked at them. I kicked off my boots and laid across my bed. They started filing out, except Sam. She tried to figure out my deal, but I wasn't in the mood. My grief had turned to uncontrollable rage.

"Sam, leave the boy be. We'll talk to him tomorrow when cooler heads prevail." She huffed loudly, expressing her disappointment.

Stand in line.

After a while, I sat in darkness. I'm too amped up to sleep, but I'm sure none of the bunnies want anything to do with me after how I handled Poppy.

She was trying to help; she was the only one who knew, and I pushed her away. See, I didn't need all this drama, just sex and booze. I had a bottle stashed in my room, and I could take care of my other needs. I rubbed one out so I could close my eyes on this nightmare of a fucking day.

My mother was dead, and I was alone.

I woke up knowing I would have to own up to my actions. I was grief-stricken about my mother, but I had a dream about her, and it seemed to ease my mind. She was pain-free and back to her joyful self and beautiful radiance. At peace, like she wanted.

I got up and dressed, heading to breakfast, but saw everyone was gone, and a lone plate was on the counter. I ate, then took my bike for a ride. I wish the drive helped, but it only amplified the screams in my head. I turn around and follow a path once shown to me until I end up at Poppy's childhood home. A part of me hoped she would be there, lying on a blanket in the sun, but it was only me.

I set my stand and hop off. I didn't have a blanket but sat near the water, listened to nature, and hoped the door to Heaven opened to give me a sign.

I spent a few hours there before returning home and resuming my old role as the black sheep. But before I do, I need to stop...at Throttle and talk to my old friend Mickey.

"Fiend, I thought you'd be clean by now since it's been so long since your last re-up. Unless..." He looked me over and chuckled, "you picked up some extras when you came bursting in looking for Frankie. He was in the middle of inventory before I ran out. I know that for a fact."

I didn't have to say anything; he could feel my guilt. I sit down, and he pours me a beer. "It's okay, no harm, no foul. If I were an addict, I'd take advantage. Judging by the time since I last saw you, you took more than a handful! But now the gravy train has run out, and here you are, ready to do business with Mr. Sebastien."

I remain quiet because all I want to do is wipe that smirk off his face, especially for calling me an addict.

"To get anything, you first have to meet with him."

"Why would he need to meet with me?"

He pulls a glass to dry. "That's how new referrals go. Them's the rules."

"Referral? How could I be referred?"

He smirked, "I told him about all of Frankie's prior customers. He was very intrigued when he found out about you, and that's before your boss came scouting for work."

That's why he said my name during the introduction.

"Let's get this bullshit over with." He gestures to follow him, and we end up in the back at the end of a dark hall-way. He knocked three times, then peeked his head in. "Hey, boss. He's here." He nodded, then opened it wider for me to pass through. I didn't even know there was a back part to the bar. I slip past, and he closes the door almost imme-diately.

"Hola, Senor Fiend. It's nice to meet you in person. More

personally than the group introduction. You and I are going to be great acquaintances."

"And why is that?" His sugary, sweet persona was getting on my nerves.

"I heard that you developed a... craving and... that it is a secret you are keeping from the group. A dirty little secret."

He reaches into the desk drawer and pulls out these blue pills. "These aren't those little blue pills you use to get rock hard. You look like you don't need those as a young viral man, but it is a bonus to the euphoric high it provides. I call them blue magic. And this has a bonus, it hits in less than five minutes. Almost instant gratification."

Now I knew he was bluffing, I always had to wait at least 10-20 minutes, I'd take that time for foreplay, and by the time she came I was ready to get mine.

I crossed my arms. He tosses me a pill that I could barely see mid-air, "Here, on the house. You'll see, I don't lie about my product." The pill was a perfect circle, not like a regular pill shape. It looks like those sweet-tart chewy candies.

He taps his watch, "I can time it for you." I open my timer app, "No thanks, I can do it myself." I take the pill back and start the timer.

"Now, as you wait, I have a proposition for you. I aim to become the biggest and most powerful drug kingpin on the Eastern coast! When people need their fix, they should come to the one and only untouchable Sebastien Aviarro!"

I scoff, "Do you talk to hear yourself, or are you truly this self-centered? What do you need me for? We're already running your supplies."

"Yes, my supplies, not my weight. My product is not getting out as far as I need it to topple these mediocre cartels. I was the #1 seller in Cuba, and this is my expansion! I'm going to be a worldwide name."

"I'm not helping you." I flat-out respond. He checks his watch, "Oh, but you will...because right about now, that pill has hit your system."

And he was right; it was as if I had taken a deep breath of the purest air. I could run a marathon, mow the entire property to the tree line, and still have the energy to fuck two or three bunnies.

"Whoa!" I squeeze my hands and shake my head. I wasn't going to say it, but these had way better effects than Frankie's version. I'd only need one for any circumstance and could pace out my doses.

"So, we agree you will conduct and pass the inspection so I can build my empire?"

"Absolutely not. Nothing you say will get me to change my mind."

He turns and grabs a remote and points it to a screen. It shows four surveillance camera footage, including my talk with Mickey, but even worse, the live feed of us, including me, watching myself on the screen. He rewinds the tape to the moment he tossed the pill, and I took it.

CHAPTER TWENTY-TWO

HOOKED
THE MERCILESS FEW MC: DEVIL'S IGNITED
Briarswood, Mass.

It was a setup.

I couldn't even get mad; had I not restarted popping pills, I wouldn't even be here. Teddy's words echo in my head: You still have to work hard to continue your sobriety. Don't get lax. I didn't get lax; I became weak and relied on those pills to numb my pain and avoid all my problems.

This was a problem I couldn't run from.

"So you see, Senor Fiend, you will help me unless you want this footage to wind up in the hands of

your brothers. What would they think? You'd be a failure. But think of it like this: you'll be helping many people like yourself get the relief they need. So, make sure it clears the inspection, and I'll keep this little gem tucked away for safekeeping. Deal? I don't see any other way out if you want your dirty little secret safe."

I was grinding my teeth to diffuse my anger; although I felt euphoric with the drugs, I was feeling too many feelings at once. What choice did I have? I was against the wall.

He holds out his hand, and I shake it. He tosses a bag my way, and by instinct, I catch it. I'm on my way home to face my family.

I walk right into Lila swinging at me; if my senses weren't heightened, she would have slapped the shit out of me. These girls can throw a mean hook.

"You bastard, what the fuck is wrong with you? Huh?! That'll be the last goddamned time you put your filthy hands on her again! I never expected you to be abusive!"

She was swinging for the fences; honestly, I couldn't blame her. All the bunnies had her restrained, but they wanted to tear me apart, too. I wasn't an abuser; I never wanted to be seen that way.

"Alright, that's enough. Everyone calm down now!" Sam stands between me and the mob. "I want an explanation for yesterday, and I want it now. I do not tolerate abuse of any kind, Jett."

By then, everyone was glaring at me. This is what I feared if they found out about my addiction. I was living my nightmare on a different subject. I felt guilt and remorse, especially because Poppy wasn't there. Judging by her words, I don't know if she'll ever come back.

I ruined her, but not in a good way. Is this who I am when I'm desperate? Or when somebody tries to help me. I had not dealt with the blow that my mother was gone. I know it doesn't excuse what I did.

I looked around and saw anger and confusion on their faces, except Sam; I saw the same concern that Poppy was trying to show me. She stepped forward and took my hand. "Tell me what happened. We're your family, Jett."

She sounded exactly like Mom, and the lump in my throat was choking me. I couldn't catch my breath. It was a force cleansing, and I let it all go.

"She died, Sam! The cancer won, and my mom is dead! I can't think, I don't know how to feel, and the one person who wanted to help, I just...snapped, and I never meant to hurt her!" Nothing worse than feeling weak and crying. I thought they would leave me there, but instead, I felt my brothers pick me up, and everyone surrounded me. The girls squeezed in between and comforted me. After what seemed like an eternity, I felt them release me, and I saw a few girls wipe away tears.

Lila stayed near, "I'm sorry I swung at you, and I'm sorry about your mother. I didn't know."

"None of you knew except Lucifer and Sam. Poppy went with me. That's why I was gone. I went after I found out she was in home hospice. In my heart of hearts, I knew, but she was so energetic after a day of visiting. She said that seeing me gave her peace, peace to pass on. Now...weeks later, she's gone and doesn't want me to come home! She said my home was here, but I should have been there; I should have been there!" Lucifer pulled me into him, and he slapped my back hard, and it released more tears.

"I'm sorry, son. She's no longer in pain; like she said, she's at peace. Now, you have to accept and move forward. Continue to make her proud."

Make her proud? By attacking a club girl and threatening her, by making a deal with the devil so he too can keep my addiction a secret? What's there to be proud of?

I needed to take this as a sign to reevaluate my life. "I'm

sorry I exploded. I didn't handle any of this properly. I understand if you hate me."

"No one hates you, boy. We didn't know what you were going through. I went through hell with Frankie, physically and emotionally. I also didn't know what to do with all these emotions. I was lucky to have Avi, and it may not look like it, but you have the same support."

I sigh, "She hates me. I may not have hit her, but I scared her enough that she thinks I'm not worth saving." I glanced at the girls, and by their expressions, I was right.

Poppy wasn't coming back.

Lucifer's phone rang, and he stepped away. I sat down, and Sam sat close, one hand on the back of my neck and the other holding my hand.

"We have to go. Sebastien has two trucks heading to the state line. Fiend, you stay here. We can go without you this time. Take some time off."

I jumped up quickly, "No, I need this distraction. I can do this." He consented, and we all went into the basement to suit up.

The real reason was if I didn't show up, Sebastien could spill my secret, I had screwed up

enough. I had to do my job and clear the shipments."

Two short white trucks meet us when we get to the docks. Lucifer approaches the driver, who hands the manifesto to him. To my relief, Sebastien isn't there, but even the look on the driver's face makes me think he knows. I can't trust anyone who works for him.

"Let's see. We got two different destinations: the Rhode Island state line and the Vermont state line. Our Rhode Island chapter will pick up, and a group called the Indestructibles will carry the Vermont load. Who wants to check the trucks?"

"I'll do both!" It sounded too eager, so I dialed it back. "It'll keep my mind busy. I can get it done in less than 15."

He hands me the clipboard, "Be thorough and take as much time as you need. Do you want someone to assist?"

"No, it's fine."

"Alright. We'll map out the route and who goes where."

I slip my gloves on and walk to the back of the first truck. The supplies are stacked to the roof with a pathway to the back. There were boxes of feeding

tubes and pumps, masks, gloves, sterilizers, and syringes. I counted the number of boxes and noticed six were not listed; they must have been in there. I lift the corner of one and feel the total weight of the box, much heavier than medical supplies. It must be a couple of kilos. I lean down to read the label that mimicked the others.

"Supplemental baby formula." I scoff.

"Everything good?" I'm startled when I see Demon on the gate of the truck. He had one foot on the threshold as if he were going to step in. I step toward him. "Yup," I initial the list, "good to go." He steps down and I check the other the same way, and this also had extra boxes but ten instead of six. This was the one going to Vermont, and I felt...irritated. He knew it was my home state and couldn't wait to flood the new territory with his product. Then I immediately thought of Katy or Chelsea succumbing to it like mom under the pressure of raising Kat or Dog, but it was far-fetched. But there was this stab of uncertainty. They shut the doors as I joined the group.

"Fiend and Wicked will head toward Vermont since that's your territory, and you know the way. Reaper, Demon, and I will take Rhode Island. Here's the information on the Inde-structibles: they sound like a version of the Ace of Spades. Look for a man named Jaguar."

"Right, Boss." It was four hours to the border town listed

on the directions. It was about two and a half hours south of Haverhill. I know because I passed it on my way back last time. Nothing was there; it was obviously a shell to distribute to nearby towns and cities. I was heated by how close it was to home, like he planned it. I know dealers like him don't care how their drugs affect society but that they come back for more.

I took the head, and Wicked took the rear. It was pitch black as most towns relied only on a handful of lights to illuminate their tiny space, and the roads in between were provided the bare minimum. It felt like Mad Max after dark. I was on high alert because an ambush could come from anywhere. However, I'm unsure how well Sebastien is known in these parts.

After an uneventful trek, we arrive at an abandoned gas station. The truck pulls up, reverses back into a spot, and turns his lights off. Not sure if it's safe or smart. I pop my kickstand but leave her running.

"Ayo, Fiend." Wicked gets my attention as he parks beside me but turns his engine off. "I'm sorry about your mom. I want you to know I'm here if you need to vent. I can take time away from Priya and Tamla. I've been considering letting them go anyway, man. I want to be wild and free, like you."

"Huh, trust me, I am not a good example of anything. Besides, those girls trust their relationship with you enough to share you with others. Think about their feelings before you dump them. Are things getting serious? And that's why you're panicking, wanting to run. Don't do that; be open and honest. They are sweet and understanding girls. They don't deserve mistreatment."

"When'd you get so philosophical?"

"When I messed up a good thing by not giving it what it needed to grow." I sigh, thinking about her.

Wicked didn't respond; he knew what I meant. Every mile down this road to get here made me think of her, what I did, and what I should have done differently. I'm brought out of my thoughts by a low hum that turns into engines running, and we see the lights coming from the North.

"On your toes!"

The lights turn into the lot. I'm counting six of them versus the three of us, and the driver isn't reliable; he'd turn on whoever to save his life. It was two against all.

The lead guy looked younger, more in our age range than the boss man. They must be a newly formed club. The leader slicks his hair back before setting his kickstand and dismounting. He straightens his leather vest, and I barely make out two lines of script: Jaguar and Captain.

It's time to hand off the dirty shipment.

"You Jaguar?" He stops in front of me, offering his hand. I shake.

"Aye. This is Bear, Fox, Moose, Goose, and Frogger. We are the Indestructibles of Hyatt County."

"Nice to meet you. I'm Fiend, and this is Wicked from the Merciless Few Devils Ignited Massachusetts chapter."

"Wait! THE Merciless Few?!" The young blonde on the left says, then gathers his composure to keep cool. "I heard great things about you guys. Why would you take a dirty job like this?"

I tense up because they know what's in this shipment. And Wicked did not. "A job is a job. The driver has the manifesto. Once you take ownership, we can leave. Pleasure doing business with you."

"And you as well. Hey, who do we talk to about wanting to become a Merciless Few chapter up here?"

"Headquarters is located in the Maryland chapter; you can request with them and start the process; that's all I know."

"It takes two to three years to go through the approval process, gain the charter, and officially call yourself a Merciless Few club chapter. Good luck." Wicked adds.

Jaguar chuckles, elbowing his brother, "Guess we don't have to be as squeaky clean as I thought."

I knew what he meant. I signaled for us to leave and head back to the clubhouse.

I never wanted to sleep so much in my life. I was super sore and decided to take some pain relievers instead of the blue magic.

We ran jobs for Sebastien and a few others who utilized the docks for the next four weeks. It felt like it was non-stop work but in a good way. I was more than halfway to my goal. I could buy the stock option of my dream bike right now, but I wanted a custom cerulean blue paint with a white swirl. It would look like the galaxy and stars, and I would get 'Destiny' etched on the side. I would also pay for an upgrade on the horsepower. Altogether, it was an extra $15,000 with labor. Now, I thought about every job as another notch toward my goal. Although technically I had the money from my parents, I didn't want to use it because it solidified that they were gone.

It was blood money.

CHAPTER TWENTY-THREE

HOOKED
THE MERCILESS FEW MC: DEVIL'S IGNITED
Briarswood, Mass.

My nights were filled with club business, but the days were empty and quiet. I cleaned my room and put all her stuff into the bottom drawer, and now I have a drawer full of memories. I wasn't deaf to the whispers when I passed the girls; they were still social. They weren't trying to avoid me, but they weren't talking loudly about what was happening at the bunny house, as usual. One day, curiosity got the best of me. It was a great day to barbecue; the grill was going, and I helped out between the kitchen and the grill.

"Girl, is Patricia still messing with Van from the Ace of Spades?" Lil asks as she, Lacy, and Rose share a tub of birthday cake ice cream.

"Nah, since their new leader came into power, it's been hell on their girls. They're a little liberal on sharing and not necessarily asking. They're making it a part of their initiation to 'bang a bunny' in front of everyone."

"Eww, how barbaric. I don't understand why Poppy went back." Then, someone dropped their spoon. I think they forgot I was around. I turned to face them, "What did you say?"

Lacy's face paled, and Rose slapped her hand over her mouth. She definitely wasn't supposed to say anything. Lila, the veteran, shakes her head—rookie mistake.

"I'm sorry, I wasn't supposed to say that out loud! She's going to kill me!"

I know it's not what I think; she can't be that stupid. I take a deep breath to disperse my anger physically. "It's fine. Can someone please tell me what's going on with her?"

They all exchange looks; some look like they want to say, and others are still pissed at my barbaric display.

"Dude, why should we even bother when it's obvious you never gave a damn about her! I'm not saying her current situation is better, but she got the attention she wanted. The attention you had so much trouble giving!"

I sigh and sit at the dining table and see her face soften. I think she took pity as she jokingly sat on my lap. "Careful, Lil. It's been a while. I could pop a boner at the slightest touch."

"That is not my problem. I have a man to take care of me, so keep your boners to yourself. I want you to be open and honest with me, okay?"

"Okay."

"Did you start having feelings for Poppy?"

I finally had to say it out loud in front of people, "I always did."

"Did you let her stay in your room? She mentioned it quickly, but we never asked anything beyond that."

"She said she felt protected here. I never hesitated to keep her safe, especially after hearing what happened at the bunny house."

She punched my arm, and then there was sadness in her eyes. "Then I'll tell you, but it's not good news. I don't know if she told you about her ex, but he returned and is now the Ace of Spades president. After what I heard, I'm trying to convince Everett to leave and come here, but he says it's dangerous for him...possibly even deadly."

I heard about those types of clubs; they jump you in, and you take a blood oath. The only way to leave is by spilling blood or dying. It's extreme if you ask me, but back to what she said, "You mean the spineless bastard who made that scar on her face?!"

I roared up, almost dropping her. I was heated, pacing the floor because I could feel myself about to go nuclear. Lil tried to put her hands on my chest, but she could barely reach it with her small stature.

The pats brought me out of my murderous thoughts.

"It seems he apologized and promised her that he would make her his ol' lady if she did right by him for an undisclosed amount of time. You hurt her more emotionally than he did physically, and she did what she thought was best. The lesser of two evils."

"How is an abuser better than me?"

"Abusers are crafty; they manipulate their victim to think the other option is worse. You know, saying things like you'll never find anyone to love you like I do or anything that tears her down, so she feels like it's her last chance. It's him or being alone forever."

"How could she...give up on me so easily?!"

Lila huffed, "I know you're talking out of your ass now. Did she give up on you? Really?! I remember her words after she first met you, she said, 'Wow, Lil. My heart is beating a mile a minute!' Then she giggled whenever you came around, but I'm sure you don't remember."

"Purple butterfly-shaped clip and two green bobby pins. That's what she had in her hair. It was the only thing I could concentrate on instead of staring at her ocean-blue eyes. I got lost in them and thought I was no good for her. I put a wall up, but I remember that clip, those pins, and those eyes."

Lila put her hand on her heart, "Oh my gosh, why were you such an asshole to her?!"

"Because I'm stupid, Lil. But she never stopped trying, and eventually, she wore me down. And now..." I can't believe she would let him manipulate her like this. I run my hands through my hair.

"Listen, don't fret yet. We'll do some recon and gather information. But you can't go in guns blazing into their spot. You could get caught, hurt, and killed! There may be hope for you yet. I swear you and Reaper are going to be the death of me. If I have to do this with Wicked or Demon, I'll blow my brains out, but Demon's such a manwhore it'll take the hand of God to change him. Tam, Priya, you're on your own with your man. Lila's relationship services are closed indefinitely!" We all shared a chuckle, and surprisingly, they all gathered to hug me.

They separate, and I run my fingers through my hair again, "So, uh, if I could ask. I am a bit pent-up. Does anyone want to indulge in a pity fuck? Hmm?"

A shower of rolled eyes and groans rang out as they all walked outside. It was worth a shot.

My mind was 100% with her, and I wanted to feel as good as I did when I was with her. I took a blue magic and jerked to the memories of the sounds of her calling me and moaning while I wrapped one of her pretty black lace thongs around my dick and another around my hand to inhale her. I jerked off until I was empty and sure about my intentions.

It was another week of multiple deliveries for Sebastien; he was trying to get as far and wide as possible within these few short months, hundreds of miles racked up on our bikes and bodies. I didn't know how much more I could physically take. We usually didn't do drop-offs on Sundays, which was great because we needed at least one day of rest. Bossman was proud of how much money we were earning. Sam started talking about renovations to the clubhouse, like expanding the kitchen area and a decent coat of paint. She joked about robin egg blue or canary yellow, but she kissed her man and said she was kidding. She said a color that matched the surrounding forest, like a burnt sienna or walnut color. You could see the excitement when he said whatever she wanted.

I had to make a self-run to Throttle to re-up. Mickey was not standing there cleaning his millionth glass when I walked in. Instead, I noticed the guy was wearing a leather cut, and there was a patch I couldn't make out from this distance. There are two other groups that can be categorized as motorcycle

clubs, and one is the Ace of Spades. Now that I know what kind of man their leader was, I felt hatred toward them all—birds of a feather.

I walk up to the bar, "Where's Mickey?" The guy looked irritated by my question until he peeped my patch. He adjusted his attitude and stance, pulling a glass from under the bar. "Mickey is no longer employed here. What can I do for you?"

"I need Mickey for my usual. Only he knows what that is."

I heard someone coming down the hall, and Sebastien peeked around the corner. "Hola, Mr. Fiend, follow me. Your timing is impeccable." I walk into his office, now that I think about it, I have yet to walk back into that glass case inside the apartment building. I wonder if it was a front or if they used it for other things, such as storage.

When I walked in, I saw a tall blonde with hair slicked back

and wearing the same cut as his buddy at the bar. We got along
with any and every one, but this new power regime at the Ace
of Spades is trouble. And I know the minute I recognize that
piece of shit leader, it'll take the hand of God to get me off
of him.

"Please, sit, *por favor*." I keep my eyes on Slick as I slowly
take my time sitting. He glared at me like I had wronged him
somehow; maybe he knew I was the name she was screaming
instead of his. Either way, with my lack of medication, his
presence is bothering me.

Sebastien looks between us and tuts, "Caballeros (gentle-
men), there is no need for the anger I feel in this room. Soon,
we will be working together on the biggest delivery to date. I
will work out the logistics; soon, your clubs will be wealthy
men. I am paying out $50,000 each for the safe delivery of my
cargo. Fiend you will clear the 'supplies' and as a prepay-
ment..." He tosses an item my way. It's at least a month's
supply of what I need. "No charge." The bag lands at the edge
of his desk right in front of me. I lean forward and slide it off
the desk.

Nothing is ever free.

"The order will arrive in three or four days. If we have no
more to discuss, I must talk business with my new partner
here." He sounded very dismissive toward me, and Blondie
smiled, but I didn't give a shit. I got what I needed. Looks like
we'll be doing our first collaboration, and the price was good...
almost too good.

When I returned, the house was in its usual party mode,
except it was a birthday party. A big giveaway was the banner
and streamers. It takes me a moment to realize that it was the
boss man's birthday. Luckily, I purchased this pretty nice
watch already. A Hamilton Khaki Field Mechanical Watch. I
noticed he only wore two watches; the one Sam gifted him at

their wedding reception and one that used to be his father's. It was a timeless silver mariner, but after so many repairs, it was now displayed in a black velvet box in his room. I noticed it when I spoke to them about Mom. He said he wouldn't risk losing it on a ride. I paid extra to inscribe it, 'To Our Merciless and Fearless Leader.' I went to my room and grabbed it from the top of my dresser when I noticed the bottom drawer slightly opened. I reached down and saw it was now empty. All her clothing was gone. Did she sneak in while I was out? Or did she ask one of the girls? I would have to ask later, but Sam yelled for us to sing Happy Birthday.

"Come on now! Let's show Bubba some love!" When I step out, she's lighting the candles and forcing him to sit in front of the cake.

"Baby girl, this isn't necessary. We could have had our own celebration in our room." She rolls her eyes and bends down to kiss him. "Who says we won't? Humor me because you love me, and your family loves you."

He looks at her and then shrugs his shoulders in defeat. She leans down and whispers, causing this massive smile on his face. We all know that smile.

The sheet cake is filled with candles and reminds me how old he is. We all start to chuckle without saying a word.

"When you get my age, every birthday will have meaning."

"Wise words from an old man!" Wicked blurts out, but Sam is close enough to smack him upside the head.

"Oww, Sam!"

"Show respect; I raised you better."

That's all she had to say.

"Aww, don't worry, baby girl, these boys keep an old man young."

We sang Happy Birthday, and he blew out the candles. He cut the cake, and after that, we presented our gifts. Naturally,

Wicked gifted him a fishing pole because they're avid fishers. "It's the Penn Battle III." Wicked said, but only Lucifer knew what that meant as his eyes bucked. "No way, this is one of the best in the world. Thank you, Asher. We have to go out this weekend and break her in."

"Hell, let's go in the morning!" They both lit up like kids at Christmas.

Reaper hands him a card, and inside are two VIP tickets to a Guns N' Roses concert. I remember hearing about it on the radio; those were not cheap.

Demon gifts him a Harley Davidson gift card, which goes well since he rode a custom edition 105th anniversary edition Harley. A beauty in her own right, paying homage to the ones before her, and the candy apple paint job made her all the rarer. Occasionally, when we're at gatherings, people offer to pay good money for his one-of-a-kind girl, but we all know he would never sell her. He'd bury her on the right with Sam on his left. He would spend eternity with both his girls.

"You boys sure know how to make an old man feel special."

I step forward, "Hope you like it." He takes the red leather box from me. Sam stands behind him as he cracks it open. They both gasp, "Jett, wow...this is...such a nice watch." He takes it out of the box and hands it to Sam while he takes off his current one. They switch, and she helps put it on. "Nice pick, Jett; Bubba needed a new one and bad."

"It wasn't that bad."

"The grace of God was holding onto it. I understand you wanted to wear it for me because of our wedding, but you would have kicked yourself had you lost it! And I would have kicked you, too! Now you can display it like your dad's, you hear me?"

He growled, pulling her into his lap, "Yes, darling." He bombarded her with kisses, and everyone left the immediate area. I walked outside and inhaled the cool air. It felt good. I was dreading the call for the mass shipment and betraying my brothers by going against my word and not flagging the drugs. I had overlooked so many other shipments before this one; what was another? But something felt off, and it wasn't my usual gut feeling or guilt. I couldn't figure out what was worse because if I confessed now, they wouldn't trust me again, and the regret would have been more than I could bear. I mean if I lose them...what else do I have? My siblings don't need me. They miss me, but they've been doing fine. And Lucifer's words about how he frowned upon drug use, but we were adults, rung in my head.

I need help.

I can't do it on my own.

And my peace is gone.

She's your peace, Jett. You do right by her. Mom tells me in one of our conversations. Great, I've let down my dead mother. A part of me is still upset with her wishes, but I have granted them. Kat told me they would have eternity jewelry made for all of us. It's when you incorporate a bit of your loved one's ashes. I requested a chain so that I could have her near my heart.

These were all emotions I had not dealt with; I ignored them and numbed them with drugs. I was going down a dangerous path and doing it alone. I had done some research and found a facility about 30 miles west of here that helps with addiction. No solution didn't end with them finding out. So why go through with the big shipment? For two reasons: to keep them safe and in Sebastien's good graces. Once I'm admitted, he won't hesitate to squeal, but by then, they will know. And because they need the money. Fifty grand could keep the club running for at least a year, if not more.

"Ahem." I look over and see Lila and Kitty. They sit on the swing, and I lean against the post.

"We have a problem, Fiend. There was...an incident, and we haven't seen Poppy since." I was happy the girls were staying together, safety in numbers, but not if that place wasn't safe. I wonder if I can take part of my share in the insurance policies, and we can set up an addition here. And with that, I would get Poppy back home.

Where she belongs.

With me.

CHAPTER TWENTY-FOUR

HOOKED
THE MERCILESS FEW MC: DEVIL'S IGNITED
Briarswood, Mass.

Back to the present, I was already seething but trying to be calm. "What happened?" Kitty looked concerned about telling me what was happening in the bunny house.

"Before you go completely unhinged like Reaper, I texted her this morning, and she replied, I think she's okay. Remember she went back to Bryan after what happened here? He played the perfect gentleman for a while before he showed his true intentions, but this time, he threatened to kill her if she left. He's resumed the physical abuse along with the verbal. The last time I saw her, she said she made a huge mistake and overreacted in your room. She said you were going through so much, and she nagged you one too many times. She said she deserved it, that you should have hit her. I knew those were Bryan's words, not hers. He's beaten her down so much in such a short timeframe she doesn't think she's worthy of anything. I'm scared, Fiend...of what I don't know."

"She's not at the bunny house?" They shook their heads. "After he pledged to do right, one of the stipulations was that she had to live at the Ace of Spades house. He's essentially cutting her off from us and doing God knows what! I'm terrified of what he's doing to her or making her do. You heard about their initiation process."

My mind conjures up all these worst-case scenarios. I couldn't go in guns blazing, especially when we had to work with them soon. This douchebag was at the top of my shit list now, and I WAS getting her back.

"Keep me updated if she contacts you, especially if she asks for help. If she does, all bets are off, and I'm going to prison if I have to, anything to save her. We'll have to work with them soon; let me observe so I know what action to take. If push comes to shove, I'll tell you where my debit card is to bail me out."

"Are you going to tell the guys?"

"This is my fault and my problem. I caused this, and I'm going to fix it." Lila stands and touches my arm, "You need to prepare for the worst. She may have physical bruises in addition to the emotional abuse. She may not be the sweet girl hanging around for the tiniest bit of attention from you. I want you to look me in the eye and promise me you'll do right by her! I mean it!" Lil is not a girl who cries; she's tough as nails, but she's like any girl when it comes to love. She knows my long-standing stance on emotion, feelings, and even love. I loved my mother and my family. She angrily wipes away the tears, looking anywhere but at me. Kitty observes everything but with no emotion except fear. She was worried about Poppy's current condition. I'm sure all the girls were.

I pace the porch, "It's insane! No matter how much I

pushed her away, a small part of me always wanted to protect and have her around. After she told me those awful stories about her ex from then on I was happy to see her because I knew she was safe. Now... God help that bastard because anything done to her, I'll triple it. I'll gladly sacrifice my life for hers if she lives in peace."

That did it, and now Lil's crying profusely. I grab and hold her. She playfully shoves me away, "Okay, enough of your comforting; just my luck that Everett shows up to see you holding me."

"He's not...is he?"

"Please. I'd cut his balls off and toss them in the garbage disposal. You crazy bastards practically raised me. I wish I could have done something to stop this."

"This is my burden to bear. I'll spend every day groveling at her feet if I get her home. I'll never let her out of my sight."

"Could my stubborn ass of a brother finally be ready to say that he likes her? It's okay to admit. Take baby steps." She laughed as she punched my arm, but I kept my stance. She notices I didn't laugh, and it becomes an awkward silence until I groan and run my fingers through my hair, pulling at the ends. I give up trying to hold it in, "I fell in love with her, Lil. Okay!" Kitty looked understandably shocked, but Lil smirked. I'll never hear the end of it, but I couldn't deny it, especially lying in bed every night thinking of no one but her. She was in my dreams, my nightmares, and in my heart. I had to admit, "She's my peace, Lil. I need her."

"Then you got to bring her home." Kitty agrees. I'm going to suggest we build our own bunny house. These aren't just girls who hang around. These proud, dedicated women cared for us to show they appreciated us. There's nothing more loyal than that, and we owe them so much.

"Fiend!" Someone from inside calls for me. Lil grabs my wrist, "Bring her home, please."

I head in, see Wicked head down to the basement, and follow. Lucifer is leaning against the table, staring at us. I could tell he was trying to process whatever he was trying to say to us.

"We got a job, but this time it's different."

"How so, Boss?" Reap asks.

"First, we'll be working with the Ace of Spades on this job. There will be four deliveries at once."

"Aye, but there's five of us. We can each take one, and you'll ride with one of us." Demon says, and they all agree, but I knew what he would say next.

"He doesn't think a single man is enough to guard a truck, so we'll be in groups of two and one group of three."

"This is stupid! Why can't he deliver two at a time? That way, we're not sharing our bounty with some mediocre copycat." Demon was not for the sharing.

"Trust me, I suggested, but he was adamant about all four trucks getting to their destination simultaneously. He calls it 'on the job training,' especially if we have to do multiple runs such as this, plus... each group receives $50,000 once the job is complete."

"$50,000?!" Everyone screamed in shock. Lucifer confirms. "Exactly. We may not be hard up on money, but that's a pretty good chunk for each of us even after the percentage toward the group pot."

"For medical supplies?" Reaper responds, understandably suspicious.

Lucifer shrugs, "Suppose so. As always, we'll check them before anybody leaves to go anywhere. The trucks will be ready tomorrow night, and we meet him and the Spades at 10 pm. So rest up. Tomorrow will be a long night, especially since I don't have the final locales yet. I should get that by text before 9 am tomorrow. If you'll excuse me, I'm going to indulge in a little birthday treat called my sweet Samantha."

He grinned, and all I could do was shake my head. I lay in my bed thinking, fantasizing but also getting

flashes of what I might do if she's been abused. I would go into an irreversible black-out rage, something I couldn't come back from until there was blood on my hands. For her, it'll be worth it. She deserves the world, and I'll do my best to give it to her.

My hand slides up and down my chest and stomach, and I remember when the piercing touch of her nails raked across me, giving me goosebumps. I put my other hand behind my head. I never found out who came into my room and cleared her drawer. I resumed fantasizing about my sweet girl and all the ways I would claim her, including the way she wanted most, verbally. Hell, I'd scream it to the heavens.

I resumed sliding my hand until it rested on top of the fabric covering my throbbing dick. I was so focused on the fantasy in my head that I thought it was her. My eyes shot open, and I sighed frustratingly. It was so hard thinking about the girl who tried to suck my soul out repeatedly with this incredibly sexy gaze as she did it. It was too much; I needed her. Not just for sex but to feed my heart and soul. I would worship her, so she knew she was all I needed. "Poppy." I moaned while trying to replicate how she made me feel. I loved the way she twisted her hands as she worked me to orgasm. I mimicked and felt that familiar tingle. I remember when I started preferring her over other girls and stopped sharing myself with anyone.

That time she saw Kitty in my room. I saw her try to keep

calm and not look like that girl, the jealous type. And even though she didn't, I felt my stomach drop even though I pretended not to care. She saw right through me. That's why she persisted; she saw my walls crumbling.

God, I love her so much. I fell asleep and dreamt of her.

CHAPTER TWENTY-F

HOOKED
THE MERCILESS FEW MC: DEVIL'S IGNITED
Briarswood, Mass.

We finally got all the logistics for the run on Friday night. We'd meet at a secret location at 10 pm. Sebastien never said what the rules are about coming strapped, so we suited up as usual. I stowed an extra weapon on my person and my trusty twin 9mm. When I walked back up the stairs, I could see the uneasiness in Sam's eyes, "I don't like it, Bubba. Something is off about this. I thought you were supposed to keep our boys clean?" Her anxiety started to turn to anger. You know that point where you're so angry and frustrated you're on the verge of tears? That was Sam at this moment. She had one hand on her hip and the other running through her hair. She couldn't go through another jail sentence; it would undoubtedly be much longer than the last one.

"Baby girl, it's $50,000. Enough for all those renovations you wanted..."

"I don't care about the renovations if it risks your life or your freedom, Rocco!"

Ooh, his government name. Yep, she was pissed. She stormed away and slammed the door, leaving him where he stood. He sighed while wiping his face.

"Damn, woman. Let's go!" He said a bit harsher than usual. In his mind, he couldn't turn down the opportunity for such a large amount. We were still replenishing the funds, which would put us above what we started with before we were locked up.

We already had our bikes lined up outside, ready to roll. I could see the frustration, "Boss, you okay?"

"Yeah, let's get this over with. I'll start square one in the morning. This is our last ride for Mr. Aviarro. Medical supplies or not, we are too close to being pinned with his drug dealings, too. Sam's right, I can't risk it." Everyone nods, but I feel that pang of guilt because we are pinned to his drug dealings.

Now I had to clear it so that everything goes smoothly, and they would be none the wiser until after I was admitted. While they go completely legit, my time will be filled with healing and getting clean. I'm not looking forward to the detox; perhaps that and the unknown about Poppy were the reasons I had been taking the blue magics steadily for weeks now. To distract myself, to numb all the emotion and pain. Poppy was right; I didn't need them.

I needed my brothers.

And I needed her.

Lucifer revs his bike three times and looks back. Sam is outside watching him leave as she always does. She gave him a wave and a kiss, and he blew one back, and I could see the weight lifted off his shoulders. One thing he hated was when she was upset with him, but they never stayed mad. They loved each other too much to go to bed mad or leave the house angry. He finally smiled before pulling forward, and we followed. Lucifer followed his GPS's directions to an unfamiliar area. It looks like an old, abandoned mill. There are four sizeable white delivery trucks, reversed parked with their lights on; it looked like the settings for a rumble. Next to each one is a member of the Ace of Spades on his bike, except one. Looks like they were waiting on us. Their leader was the one standing; not sure if it was a scare tactic, but Boss M   an had six inches of height and about 100 pounds in mass on this guy. I was making mental notes about each of them, self-identifying features, like the twins with matching 'Mom' tattoos on their biceps or the shaggy-haired brunette with a savage scar running across his face. He utilized the waiting by playing with his switchblade. It let us know he had at least two weapons. There's no way this gang came unarmed for a drug run.

We lined up facing them and turned off our bikes; Lucifer dismounted and approached him. He held his hand out, "Lucifer, Merciless Few: Devils Ignited."

The leader, also known as Bryan, long stares at his hand then looks at him; crossing his arms, he tuts, "Huh. Name's King, Ace of Spades." He still refrains from shaking Lucifer's hand; I took that as a sign of disrespect.

Strike one...

Had I told my brothers the story about his abuse toward Daisy, past and present, this meeting would be a goddamned bloodbath. I have been entertaining the many ways I would separate his balls from his body. Perhaps a long incision under his ball sack and watch him bleed out. I'm sure it wouldn't go as I imagined but watching him suffer would be a bonus.

He was a pompous, arrogant woman beater, the very thing we stood against. Lucifer keeps his cool, "These are my boys,

Demon, Wicked, Reaper, and Fiend." He looked at everyone but kept his gaze on me, and I leaned back.

Say something, motherfucker. I goddamn dare you...

He points behind him, "My boys, Joker, Spade, Jack, Ace, and Club."

Wicked leans over, "I don't like this douchebag."

"If you only knew." He looks at me with a raised brow.

Bryan pulls a piece of paper from his back pocket, "Sebastien said you wanted to inspect the loads; here's the inventory sheet." He's too close because when his hand shoots out with the paper, it slams against Boss Man's chest, causing everyone to stand up. I accidentally rev my engine as I shoot up.

That's strike two, motherfucker...

Lucifer holds his hand up to keep us at bay. "It's alright, boys, we're good. Fiend, take inventory." He reaches back with the paper. I dismount and take the paper. "You want any help?"

I eye Bryan and his band of jokes, "Hell no. I will do it alone. I don't need any help. Give me 20 minutes, Boss."

I walk behind the first truck and see all the doors are raised. I hopped up and saw the setup was a bit different. The pathway went halfway, but I could check everything from there. I started marking off the supplies listed and was shocked that this truck was clean—no unmarked or extra boxes. I was immediately suspicious. Where were the drugs? I stood for a moment before slipping on my riding gloves. I push against a box marked masks, which doesn't give in the slightest.

Knowing that, I lifted the corner and realized it was the supply. Instead of unmarked boxes hidden away, he put them in the supply boxes in case someone wanted to accompany me. Every box I checked for weight was full of product. I'm no expert in massive drug hauls, but it was a few hundred kilos in each truck. You could indeed do some hard time if caught. I saw no reason to check the rest, but I went through the motions and burned about 17 minutes, closing the door after my inspection.

Now that they are in my presence, I gauge myself against Bryan. He was no King, and I wouldn't call him such. A King treats his Queen with the utmost respect and places her on the highest pedestal. He was an Aces of Spades clown, a clown I was going to make pay for what he did.

I pull the door down on the last truck and come around the corner to see my group off their bikes. "What's going on?" Nobody says anything.

"The shipments are good, no?" Sebastien appears from the woods. I see his black luxury SUV hidden behind the tree line. He had been watching the whole time. He steps in between our groups. "Gentleman, please, no need for animosity. You are here to do a job for me and get paid handsomely. Is the shipment in line with your rules?" He looks at me for confirmation, to confirm his lie in front of everyone. It may be dark, but the shadows formed from the lights against him give the illusion of an evil smirk.

"It's fine." I sign for everyone to see, and he claps his hands. "Perfecto! Now, Caballeros, pair up, one from each group except one group will have three unless Senor King wants one of his to stay back?"

He scoffs, "Nah, all my guys ride; my extra guy will ride with me...for safety. The King never rides alone. My boys know to protect their leader at all times. By any means..."

He announced it like it was supposed to mean something when it didn't mean shit to us, especially me.

Sebastien claps his hands, "Let's pair up and go. You get paid once all shipments arrive at the destination points."

A rev of an engine brought me out of my thoughts. I was at the end, and I looked over to see Bryan and his lackey; I didn't give a shit to remember his name. They're lined up next to me, which I found weird because club presidents usually lead their line, not trail it. It looks like taking a double dose of blue magic was working cause my senses were on high alert. The drivers of the truck hop in and start

them. Sebastien hands each team a piece of paper with what I assume is our destination. You all have eight hours, more than enough time to deliver my supplies and report back.

Bryan nudges his buddy and whispers in his ear while looking my way. Every breath he took irritated my soul, and every minute I didn't know about Poppy's condition was another strike against him. I looked down at his hand and noticed he was wearing rings on his index and ring finger. It wasn't for aesthetics because one was made from a bike chain, and the other spiked and could do damage when connected with its target.

"Hey! You take the rear, and we'll take the front."

I blankly stare at them, "Whatever." The truck rolled forward, and they headed to the front to escort it. I couldn't wait for this deed to be done so I could rescue my girl. I had to keep my composure and remain calm. I wasn't sure if he knew who I was to Poppy, but I needed to be ready for anything if he did.

Other than the shifting of the truck gears, the ride was quiet. The flame of anger dwelling in me grew every mile we rode together. It took a lot of work to see where we were going from behind. I swerved occasionally to get a glimpse of the surroundings, but all I saw was thick woods and empty roads.

Thirty minutes later, I regretted not looking at the final destination. I was relying on them and riding blind. The truck downshifts and begins to slow down, and I fall back and give him enough space. We turned down this dark road, but I saw no buildings to drop off this load. They make a right down an even darker path, and I trail even further behind the truck to make sure I can see the two of them. They make another right and park; the truck passes them and then parks so the trailer door is facing front. It was an open clearing...

A very familiar clearing...

CHAPTER TWENTY-SIX

HOOKED
THE MERCILESS FEW MC: DEVIL'S IGNITED
Briarswood, Mass.

We were just here. The meeting point that Sebastien picked. I confirmed it with all the bike tire marks. I see them still on their bikes, laughing and staring at me. Before I could get a word out, I heard the clicking of a gun being cocked.

"Get off the bike. This him, boss?" The voice says as I turn off my bike and dismount slowly, keeping my hands up. Bryan chuckles while leaning back arrogantly, "Yeah, that's the bastard who thought he could take my bitch from me. News flash, she was never yours to begin with. She whored around with you and your little group, and she paid for every indiscretion."

"What did you do to her?"

He paced a path in front of their bikes while watching me.

What could I do with his unknown buddy behind me with a gun? "Search him." He snapped, and I felt his hands across my back and arms, down and back up my torso, where he found my guns, ripping them out and tossing them to the side. He continued around my waistband and found my blade, then he kicked my feet out but didn't pat down my legs.

"You think I wouldn't find out who she was screwing with while I was away? She was being tracked the moment I left to deal with some family business. She thought she was rid of me, but I dragged her back to where she belonged. She belongs to me." His accomplice pushes me toward the center of the field. I could see the barrel out of my peripheral vision. "Fiend, Fiend, Fiend...do you know how sick I was of hearing her call your name in her sleep! Calling for you like you would be her knight in shining armor, her saving grace. All it took was a few...love taps...to fix that. She hasn't spoken your name in days. She can't say much with a busted lip, now can she?!" He laughs, and both his men laugh with him. All I saw was red.

Guess the cat's out of the bag; he knows who I am. I did a slow clap, and I could see the rage in both their eyes, more so his little lackey.

"You know what bothers me the most is that she was always so disobedient and trying to be

independent. I had to take her down a peg when she smart-mouthed me, and I fucked her enemy in front of her. Now she knows I do what I want, when I want, and her place is down on her knees."

"And that's what you call being a man, berating and putting your hands on a woman?! I knew you were a bitch before you started talking. You're a coward, a pussy who runs a mediocre club full of what I assume are also weak punk-ass boys. Because monkeys see, monkeys do, right? The Merciless Few you will never be."

His nostrils flared in response, and he stormed toward me. I disregard the gun pointed at my head that could blow my brains out. No way I was going to let some bitch hit me while I stood there. As soon as he was close enough, I swung for the rafters and connected with his jaw, as fragile as crystal. He fell to the ground, groaning.

"It isn't enough for you to corner me from my group, so you can, what? Teach me a lesson? This is not a war you want to start, sweetheart. For the Merciless Few isn't one; we are many. You fuck with one, you fuck with us all."

Bam

I felt something hit me in the back of my head, and I collapsed to the ground, fading in and out of consciousness. I could still hear them.

"Get...out the truck and...them together..." The pain was too much, and I blacked out.

Fiend...Fiend, you have to wake up. Come back to me...

I don't know how long I was out, but my head spun, and my ears rang. I shook my head, but that made it worse.

"Ugh." Then, a loud clap rings next to my face, making me jump. "There he is. He's finally back, boys. Let's get on with it." Someone says. I blink rapidly until my vision is slightly blurry but clearer than a minute ago.

I was now looking at Bryan and his three henchmen before me.

"Is this the part where you tell me your master plan, and I pretend to care?"

"No, this is the part where everything you say has a cause and effect, so I'd choose what I'd say wisely...I don't think she can take many more shots." My ears tune into a tone; it's muffled and high-pitched. Deck looks to be struggling with whomever he has in his clutches. "Come on, you filthy bitch, don't make me hurt you more than we already have." The screams grew louder and more enraged until he tossed them in the circle. My mind almost went blank when I saw the dirty, battered, and bruised body, which was motionless—those soft features and hair I recognized immediately.

"Poppy!"

"Help her up so he can see what happens when the Queen disrespects her King and becomes a Fool!" He grabs her roughly by her arm, and she fights tooth and nail. She stomps on his foot while screaming through the gag. He rears his hand upward to hit her, and she flinches. He laughs and basks in her fear.

Now, I can clearly see the girl I once knew as bubbly and outgoing. She stood there looking like she lost some weight. The multiple bruises on her legs and arms triggered me as my eyes roamed her beaten body, but it was her face, her sweet face. Those once vibrant blue eyes were dull and lifeless, surrounded in darkness; she had a black eye and a busted lip and cheek. I swear he had re-punctured that old scar she showed me. Her legs shook, and I couldn't tell if it was because of weakness or an overwhelming emotion when she saw me.

She let out this gasp that sounded like a relief to see me. Tears ran down her face and over her wounds, and I could tell they stung, but she did her best to offer me a smile of comfort over the gag. To say that, in some way, she was okay. But she wasn't. My radiant flower child was beaten and bruised, and it was my fault. She would have been safe had I not pushed her away. He made her feel like she wasn't worth anything; he took advantage when she was at her lowest, and I'll never forgive myself.

"I'm sorry, my sweet girl."

Bryan pulls his gun and aims it at me. I keep dealing with these boys who aren't man enough to pull the trigger; they want to yap yap yap about their shortcomings, and he was no different. "Oh, shut up! You're not her hero, or savior, or Romeo. You can't save her. You can't even save yourself. I'm going to get rid of you, her, and your pathetic group. Every one of my guys got their orders to execute your brothers once they were outside city limits. We started and will end this biker war and become the most ruthless, badass biker gang in Massachusetts. You Merciless Few fucks have been the talk of the town for too fucking long! It was fate that our former leader called me up a week before he was shot and killed. He was going to make me his captain."

I remember hearing about it. It was a drug run gone wrong, but that was during Frankie's reign. Who was running the club before he came back? That was a good year lapse. We didn't even know we were in a turf war because we don't give a fuck about made-up drama. "Seems the club had gone rogue with no real leader, and that's when Deck called and convinced me to come back and run it how it should be run. We are not going to be soft like you. We run this town by force; we don't ask and don't take no for an answer, isn't that right, Poppy?"

I felt my eye twitch as her breathing started to pick up as if she were hyperventilating.

Is he saying...

"Poppy knows her place. Don't you now, darlin'? She knows I chose her not because I love her. No, I chose her simply because she was the easiest to break, physically and emotionally. She could never find someone better, but she tried to fill the gap with some drug-addicted mama's boy?!"

He walks over and yanks the fabric from her mouth, and I see the extent of her busted lip. "Tell him where you belong!"

He towered over her, an intimidation tactic. "Is that how you get her to obey by threatening her with violence?"

"Stop, Jett, please! It's not a threat! It's... not...a threat." She started sobbing uncontrollably, almost hysterically.

Something wasn't right. I felt like there was no sound in the immediate area, no sign of wildlife during one of the hottest nights of the summer, only her crying. "What happened?"

"I'm so sorry. So... so sorry." She kept repeating, and I felt it. I knew she wanted to tell me something. "Look at me. Why are you sorry?"

The moment she did look at me, it made her break down again. She wasn't bound, so she fell to her knees, her arms wrapped around her stomach. "I'm sorry!" She looked at me with so much heartache. "I couldn't...I couldn't save her... I tried to hide it. I tried...so hard!"

I shook my head, whispering no over and over again. I not only lost her, but I lost a piece she was carrying within her.

She lost our baby.

CHAPTER TWENTY-SEVEN

HOOKED
THE MERCILESS FEW MC: DEVIL'S IGNITED
Briarswood, Mass.

I didn't know!

I...

"Your drug addiction was more important than her or that abomination she was carrying. I would never let her carry another man's baby! She's my property, mine!" I crumpled to my knees and then to the ground. The devastation of knowing was a pain I was not ready for.

"Jett!" She ran to me and covered me as I sobbed. I pulled myself up with all I had to see her once beautiful face. "I'm so sorry, Poppy. You didn't deserve any of this. You were better without me. I did this; I made you lose our baby!"

"See, even he said you're better with me; now get up! I'm tired of watching this soap opera bullshit. I don't want some cum dumpster as my Queen anyway. Since you want to be with him so badly. I'll make sure you watch him die before I put a bullet in your head!" He shoves her down so that she's kneeling next to me. She could hardly catch her breath, knowing she may be watching my final moments.

He may kill me, but he's not going to get away with it being a coward. I turn around, and the barrel is positioned perfectly to blow my brains out. He was speechless, "So is this what you wanted? To kill me, my brothers, the girl that I love so you can be the big bad biker gang out of Massachusetts. You, what, bribe Sebastien and convince him to put these deliveries together, and then he offers us this exorbitant amount of money, so we agree even though we have to work with this no-name knock-off club? So you isolate us and execute us one by one? You're telling me that, as of this moment, my brothers are dead?"

They all laugh, basking in the success of their plan. "Exactly, and we pocket the entire 100K!"

This was it, the end. Poppy was still facing the opposite direction, her body wracked with tears. I leaned over and kissed her on the cheek. "I love you, baby girl. Always remember that." She turned her head so fast. "You love me?"

"Always have. My regret is not telling you sooner. Every day with you was a blessing." I resumed my death stance, staring Bryan down, and I could see the hesitation. Fucking coward.

After five seconds of waiting, I shot up to my feet. "Do it motherfucker. Pull the goddamn trigger! Put me out of my misery! I lied to my brothers, betrayed them by signing off on dirty shipments, took drugs to numb my pain, lost my girl, and YOU killed my baby! I have nothing left to live for, so fucking do it! Because if you don't, I promise I'll dismember your body while you're still conscious, then light you on fire. Preparing you for the Hell you put her through." Everyone looked so shocked at my willingness to die. Call it my last rites, my confessions, so that I could maybe earn my spot in heaven with Mom and Dad.

Bang bang bang bang bang

I hear the shots, but I don't feel any searing pain, or maybe it was quick and easy.

I hear screaming, and I open my eyes to see Reaper standing over one of his guys and firing a round, the body recoils. He looks around, and I notice him holding his arm covered in blood. He was shot!

I feel like my head is on a swivel. Now I see scuffling to my left; Wicked is punching the guy. The guy is trying to defend himself, but Wicked is in a trance and wants to literally beat him to death, the blood splattering on him until Reaper pulls him off with his good arm. He pulls his gun and fires two rounds, and the piercing screams ring throughout the countryside. He hadn't executed him, but he shot him in the kneecaps. Then he started stomping on the wounds; the screams were the type that haunt your dreams. I'd sleep like a fucking baby.

Reaper, once again, had to pull him off. "You motherfucker!" He spat on him for good measure.

I immediately looked beside me to see Poppy in the fetal position, protecting herself. "Get up! Come on."

"Jett?" She hugged me immediately when I picked her up and sighed while crying.

"I go you, darlin'."

Bang bang

I heard two more shots, thinking they were getting rid of the last members, but it was I who fell to my knees. I looked down, searching for the wound, but the blood staining my shirt and growing in size was a dead giveaway. I brought

Poppy down with me when I collapsed. I suddenly had the urge to cough, and blood accompanied it.

Bang

I struggle to see Lucifer standing over Bryan, the smoke billowing from his gun.

I was wavering in and out of consciousness. They surrounded me. "Hold on, Jett! Keep that hand against the wound."

"I'm sorry. Sorry..."

"Stop talking, son, the ambulance is on the way. You're going to be okay." I looked at my family; everyone looked like they had been through a fight, Reaper was shot and Wicked's forearm had a gash on it, and he was holding his ribs. But it was her face and injuries that guilted me; she would never be the same. She would have to heal, but worse, deal with the loss of our child she tried to save.

I don't deserve them, and they no longer need to take care of me. I wasn't good enough to save. They'd be so much better if I weren't screwing up their lives.

I lifted my hand from the wound. "Jett, no!" It was the final sound I heard, along with the faint sounds of sirens.

Beep hiss beep hiss beep

Everything hurts. Everything I could feel anyway, and I realized I was alive and upset. I couldn't even do that right! What good am I to anyone?

I cough, then groan, "Ugh, why am I alive?"

"Jett?!" I see Poppy's beautiful face. She wasn't as battered or beaten as I last saw her. She was almost back to herself. She grabbed my hand and kissed it while crying. Then I saw the rest of them surrounding my bed.

"How are you feeling, son?" Lucifer asks, and all the emotions come flooding back. I snatched my hand away from her, making her jump back.

"I shouldn't be here! I should be dead! I deserve to be dead for what I put you all through!"

Sam shoved her way through and was on the other side, "You stop it! Stop it right now! Do you think your mom would want to hear you talking like that? So defeated. You are meant to be here; no matter what you have done, we are still here for you, Jett."

I shook my head, "I lied about the deliveries being clean...I sold my soul for drugs to get my fix so I could function. I even got Poppy experimenting with them. I'm a monster!"

Lucifer touched Sam's shoulder; I couldn't look at anyone. I closed my eyes. I was furious with myself and wanted them to lash out at me and give me what I deserved!

"Why aren't you angry?! Or yelling at me, telling me how much of a disappointment I am and that I don't deserve a family like you! Why...why?! JUST GET OUT!"

CHAPTER TWENTY-EIGHT

HOOKED
THE MERCILESS FEW MC: DEVIL'S IGNITED
Briarswood, Mass.

I couldn't take the looks anymore. I wanted everyone to leave me alone. Lucifer sighed and got up, "Let's give him some time, everyone. Poppy, come on, you have a follow-up doctor's appointment in an hour. Sam will escort you."

I knew Poppy would fight me on this if she didn't have to be somewhere, but she walked out without a word. Sam wrapped her arm around her as she looked back one last time.

I watched them leave one by one with Boss Man last. "We will never push you away, no matter what you think. We'll be back in a couple of days."

What for? What was the point? Then I recognized it...withdrawal. Everything and everyone was the problem, and I pointed in every direction other than where it should have been pointed: at myself.

Fuck!

My door opens, and a nurse comes in with her cart. Great, just what I need to be bothered by a stranger. She checks the chart, and I hear her gasp, "Jett Avery?"

I look to see, no way. "Miss Sadie? How are you here? Why aren't you in Vermont?" She pushes her cart closer and sits beside me. She brushes my hair, "Still as handsome as when I last saw you, but you've been shot!"

She lightly put her hand on top of the blanket covering my wounds, "What happened?"

"I'm a failure as a human and a man. I deserved this; I deserve to feel nothing but soul-crushing pain."

"Hush up, stop criticizing yourself; it does no good. You need to focus on getting better, and I will make sure you do." She checks the chart before administering the painkillers to my IV. She tuts before she grabs another syringe and sighs while pushing down on the plunger. "Why, my handsome Jett. Why did you turn to drugs?"

"How did you know?"

"It was in your blood work, and they are combating the withdrawal with low doses of Narcan since it's about out of your system."

"How...how long have I been here?"

"At this particular hospital? It's been a couple of days, but the one prior was eight or nine days; they didn't want to move you after emergency surgery to get the bullets out. They nicked a lot of veins, and you kept bleeding more than normal. Once you clotted, you were brought here to Mercy Medical."

"What was wrong with Briarswood General?"

"They don't have a dual rehabilitation program like we do. Designed to rehab your body and your mind."

"But I was supposed to go to Bravery Hearts for my drug rehab. I researched them and everything. They have what I need to get clean."

She chuckled, "They modeled their program after ours. We are their biggest sponsor. You'll get the same help but be closer to your family so they can help you through the good and bad. Tell me, how are your mom and siblings doing?"

I huff, "Better without me. Dad drank himself to death, and Mom just died of stage four cancer. My

siblings are finding a new place and selling the family home. Life's great!" I say sarcastically.

I remember Sadie always having a smile to keep me going, but not this time. She frowned and shook her head, "Who is this man before me? Not the bright young man with a future ahead of him. He's beaten down and given up. Sure, you've had some bad luck and bad news; I'm sorry about your parents, but you still have your siblings and, from what I saw, a biker family that cares for you deeply. Why has my sweet Jett given up on life?"

"You wouldn't understand. I let everyone down; I'm a failure. I couldn't save the woman who loved me from being abused! Abused so much... she..." I felt the bed rise, and I cried even harder. "She lost our baby, Sadie. I couldn't even save my baby. I don't want to live anymore. I want to die! Let...me... die..." She moved the bed barrier, pulled me forward despite my wounds, and held me. Shushing me and humming at the same time. "No, baby, it's not your time to go. You're here for a reason. That girl is your reason. You love her, right? Then you fight for her! Fight your demons and become better for her. Your fight isn't yours alone. Don't push them away; they are your family and love you. I love you! Do you hear me?! Don't you ever say those words again!" She was wiping away angry tears.

I close my eyes and cleanse my soul. As much as I am hurting, I have to pick myself up.

Miss Sadie was like a warm hug every time she came in. She introduced me to my night nurse, Miss Corrine. They both gave me positive encouragement to pull myself out of what I heard was called withdrawal depression. It's ten times worse than regular depression as the body works overtime to try and regulate the chemicals in the brain.

One day, the doctor examined my incision and cleared me from total bed rest. I pull the covers off my legs, looking down at those god-awful grippy socks and my standard-issue hospital gown. I glance at Sadie. "My ass is going to be on display."

"Ain't nobody here but you and me, and you're like a son to me, so come on. Slide off the bed slowly." I relent and slide until I feel my feet on the floor. There was a numbing electric feel as I stood. I push off a bit, and I'm standing on my own; I feel the breeze of the gown open in the back.

"Now that's a sight to see!" I hear and look back to see everyone at the door.

"Ahh, for fuck's sake!" I turn and sit down. I feel my body flush in embarrassment.

"Nice ass, Fiend." Wicked holds his stomach from laughing so hard.

"Shh! This is still a hospital. Have some manners!" Sadie scolds him. "Yes, ma'am, sorry."

She helps me back and covers me, "You remember what I told you. Open your heart." She taps her chest.

"Nice to meet everyone, I'm Sadie, his caregiver."

"Thank you for taking care of our boy, Miss Sadie."

"Take it easy on him. He holds a lot of guilt." Lucifer and Sam acknowledge. Sam looks at everyone else, and they file out. It's me and them. Sam kissed my forehead and sat down. Lucifer stood at the foot of my bed.

"Can I ask what happened after I went unconscious? How did you know what was happening?"

"Years in legal and illegal business, you know a setup when you smell it. Like when Frankie tried to get Reaper alone. The only difference is intel. I learned about his plot to eliminate us through word of mouth. Mickey got roughed up by the Aces and left for dead. He heard their whole plan while lying on the floor, fighting for his life. Apparently, to them, we were always public enemy #1. It didn't surprise me; it'll always be a one-sided fight because we're above that until you fuck with one of us. Anyway, once released from the hospital, he called me. Remember that night I told you I had to meet someone around midnight? It was Mickey. He said Sebastien let the Aces beat him, and he knew his loyalty wasn't going to keep him alive. Eventually, King and his derelicts would have him killed. He said that you had gotten into some trouble but not to press you for answers. He said you were a good kid who went down the wrong path."

Hmm, who knew Mickey would be an ally and not an enemy? I guess I owe him an apology.

"Why didn't you ask for help, son?"

"I'm so tired of being the failure, the bad egg, the black sheep. I was in an accident before I came to Massachusetts, and they gave me drugs to deal with the pain and my scar. " I pulled down the gown.

"I always wondered what caused that; it looks bad."

"I was acting out against my parents and wrapped the car around a tree. A piece of metal sliced me here. I started taking it for the pain, of course, but when I ran out, I was looking for an alternative I could use when the pain was triggered. Daisy put me onto something, and that began the start of my addiction. It's not her fault; I decided to take them. I wish I could go back."

"Things happen for a reason. Would I rather you had come to us and asked for help, of course, but sometimes we have to let our kids do stupid things to learn lessons."

"But I almost got all of us killed! Reaper got shot! Wicked has that vicious scar, and god knows what other injuries you guys sustained, all because of me."

"Bumps and bruises compared to the others."

"How did you know where I was? Are we going to have to do prison time again? Is it years this time?"

Lucifer chuckled, "You are working yourself into a frenzy when there isn't any. Once I knew the Aces plan, I put air tags on your bikes. I watched as they circled back to the meet-up spot. I had already taken care of my guy and strung him to the tree. Reaper was already shot by the time I got to him, but he had already killed his guy, and Wicked knocked his guy unconscious; he may be put into a permanent coma due to the extent of his injuries. Demon killed his counterpart only because he shoved the barrel in his mouth but didn't see Demon's pistol aimed at his heart. It was kill or be killed, and Demon shot first. It wasn't supposed to be a bloodbath, but when I saw you on the ground and how badly Poppy was hurt, I announced the 1% rule effective immediately."

Ahh, the 1% rule, 99% of the time, we were the good guys trying to do right by the world, but there are times, occasions that it goes, fuck the world, and burn it down.

"I was able to work yet another deal with the sheriff to take Sebastien down, and he and what's left of his cronies are in custody. All the trucks were taken in as evidence, and if we testify, we can avoid jail time. Everything was done in self-defense." He sighs, "It's so hard to keep you knuckleheads out of jail, but it's my fault as leader. I promise I will make better decisions for us as a whole." I could tell he was repeating what he said to Sam verbatim. She gave me a comforting smile.

"So, is bringing in the rest of the crew okay? The guys and girls are here."

"Yeah, of course."

Lucifer opens the door, and I see many relieved faces. I had so many questions. As soon as I saw her, I addressed my first concern, "Lil, was Everett hurt? I didn't see him with us, but now I'm unsure; it was dark."

She shook her head, "Everett was doing a run to northwest Maine with three other members. He's okay, and he said he's out of the Aces. He said technically, there is no more Ace of Spades."

I'm glad to hear he's okay." I look at everyone and double-check. "Where's Poppy?" The girls look visibly upset. I held my breath, waiting to know. "Sam?" I turned to her to tell me.

"She's not here. She's been through a lot, and her body shut down. She's been on bed rest since the procedure to remove the baby to prevent sepsis or infection. She took it really hard, and we've been having trouble getting her to eat, to function. We held a small ceremony and buried her near the tree line."

"Her?" My voice wavered, and I looked away as the tears welled.

"Yes, sweetie. She named her Avery Emberly Watkins."

"Avery is my middle name."

"I know, I know." She smiled through the tears.

"Oh, God! She must hate me! I ruined her life and all she wanted was my attention! She didn't deserve this, neither of them. How do I fix this, Sam?"

"You aim to get better. We will take care of Poppy until you are well enough. You have to get better, Jett. She needs you."

The door opens again, and Miss Sadie walks in, "Ahh, good

to see you are allowing the family in this time. You all should know that he's over the hump with the help of a counteractive drug. Side effects are minimal. He won't be dependent anymore, isn't that right?"

"Yes, ma'am. You all should know that she was my nurse when I had my car accident as a teenager. Because of her, I got the courage to live my dream to be a Merciless Few, and now she's helping me again to get my life together because... I fell in love."

All the girls awwed, and all the guys except Reaper and Lucifer groaned. They understood what I meant.

"And another one bites the dust!" Demon states pointedly. We all laugh, and it makes me feel again. I look them each in the eye and smile, "Thank you all for being here, forgiving me, and loving me. I didn't mean what I said last time. I have a long road ahead, but as long as I have you, I know I can do it. I love you all." And they each hug me as a sign of forgiveness.

Still, my heart wasn't whole until I laid eyes on my girl. She's gone through so much, and I need to be there for her, and eventually, we can mourn our baby girl together.

CHAPTER TWENTY-NINE

HOOKED
THE MERCILESS FEW MC: DEVIL'S IGNITED
Briarswood, Mass.

The following two weeks were the hardest; they came to see me when they could. I was at this specialty hospital that was 20 miles away. Most of our interactions were by phone, and Sam kept me updated. Poppy still wasn't mentally ready to talk to me. Sam said she was still having nightmares, but she was slowly eating more. She would sit on the swing outside, not saying a word. Then she would lay in my bed. I was relieved she was home where she should be.

My rehab was painful and arduous, but I was able to sit and stand for extended amounts of time. I was on my way to 100%. I had therapy sessions that helped me figure out why I felt so hopeless and how to deal with the feelings of so many events in my life, starting with my mother's passing.

I called Katy and Chelsea to let them know what had happened, and of course, they had a million questions and wanted to ride down to lay eyes on me. I compromised with a FaceTime call and saw the relief in their eyes. "Oh, Rocket! What happened?"

"Just a few bullet wounds, but I'll be fine. Where are Kat and Dog."

"We wouldn't let them see you like this. It's too much after Mom's death. We told them you were getting better and would call them."

"You did right by them. I should be released soon, and we can talk about a visit. I'd love to see the new house, and I know you want to see the clubhouse."

"Yes, we would! We're closer now, in a small town named Dellaton, right at the Vermont border, so it should take you less time. We also bought an RV to take road trips in. We want them to see the world before life gets them."

I understood that. There was a light knock at my door.

"We'll talk more about it later. I think it's time for my meds."

I hung up, "Come in, Miss Corinne, I know it's about time for my..." My entire brain stops functioning when I see her.

"Poppy." She didn't respond, but she came in and sat down. She was holding back all her emotions. It wasn't healthy, and she had been going through this mute phase for almost three weeks. It had to stop, and I knew I had to be the one to break it.

I hold out my hand, and she takes it, looking at our hands and not at me. I rub the soft spot between her thumb and index finger.

"Look at me. You can't keep doing this to yourself, this self-inflicted pain. It's not your fault, Poppy. None of this is. I pushed you away, I made you feel unwanted, and because of that, you endured the most unspeakable abuse: abuse you didn't deserve. You hear me? You didn't deserve it!"

She started squirming in her chair, flinching as if she was about to be hit. I place my hand on her face, tilting it up. "Say you love me, please. I'm sorry for everything. I love you, Poppy, but don't hold this in, whatever it is: sadness, anger, hate. You don't have to be strong. We'll mourn her together. From here on out, I will protect you with every ounce of me and my dying breath. I love you; say you love me, Poppy."

I pleaded, but all I got was agonizing silence between us.

"I was supposed to protect her." She whispered, then shook her head as the tears fell. I pulled her to me to hold her, and she held onto my gown as she sobbed.

"You did the best you could."

"How can you say that when our daughter is gone? I lost her."

"Stop it. Don't belittle or bash yourself for something you couldn't prevent. That bastard killed our baby, and I'm glad Lucifer took him out." I had to stop and take a breath to calm down. "They're making me talk to a therapist here, and he told me that the way to get over such a devastating loss is to do it together. He said that only we can pull ourselves out of the darkness, but I was terrified, terrified that you'd hate me!"

"Y-you told him about me?" I pull her hands up and kiss them. "Every session, you're why I'm fighting to live my new normal. That's with you, my sweet little backpack."

"Oh my God. I don't think I agreed to that being my official pet name. It's cute, so I'll let it slide. I could never hate you." That was all she said, and suddenly she smiled, and it was almost like old times again.

"I swore I would beg on my hands and knees until you forgave me for my past mistakes, for not seeing the missing piece of my heart. My mom was right. You. Are. My. Peace."

"I am?"

"You are. And I love you."

She chuckles and shakes her head, "It sounds like everything I dreamed for, and I pray it isn't a dream or illusion."

"It's not a dream." She leans forward, and finally, I feel her lips on me. Not battered, swollen, or bruised.

"Oh my Lord, is this the angel who has my Jett on cloud nine?" Sadie is grinning from ear to ear. "I finally get to see his reason for living."

"Sadie..."

She checked my vitals and IV, "I believe those were your exact words yesterday?" She knew I couldn't lie; she had a mom radar like Sam. Especially in the beginning when I screamed at her that I didn't need nothing or nobody. She called me on my bullshit when she allowed me to skip a dose of pain meds. She sat at the nurse's station until I hit the call button. She took her sweet time coming in. I was breathing like I was in labor and sweating profusely. The pain seemed to be magnified by my anger. I was damn near growling in agony, cursing under my breath.

"Don't you cut your eyes at me! I left you alone, like you said. You don't need me, so you must not need these drugs or food, huh?"

Let's say I never talked back to her again, and after the drugs set in, I apologized. She said she knew it was all my emotions combined with the withdrawal, and that's a dangerous partnership.

I rolled my eyes, "Yes, I did. Sadie, this is my Poppy." Sadie shakes her hand, "Nice to meet such a beautiful young lady. I want to tell you two a story, and if I overstep, you can let me know, okay?"

Poppy nodded. Sadie took her hand and mine, "A long time ago, probably before you were born, I fled an abusive situation. It was so bad I endured daily beatings. Then I found out I was expecting. Now, it was fight or flight. I had to get away the next night in darkness. Unfortunately, luck was not on my side. I left the pregnancy test in the bathroom garbage, and he saw it. I endured the most vicious beating. I escaped out the house's back door with nothing but my life. I ran to the nearest hospital and collapsed inside the door." Sadie wiped a tear from her eye, "I knew. I didn't want to accept it, but I knew how he viciously concentrated his blows there. I lost the baby, and things got very dark. So I understand the pain you must have gone through, and with him being here recovering, I know it didn't help. I want you to do something I didn't get to do. I want you two to visit her memorial together because it's not a grave; she lives in your heart. There is where you reflect on her short but mighty impact on your lives, how she brought mommy and daddy together. Tell her how much you love her. You are stronger than what happened, and hopefully, you'll be blessed again with a rainbow baby."

I was confused, "What's a rainbow baby?"

"It's a blessing after the loss of a child. I had a rainbow baby, my daughter, and then I had my son. Both with my husband, but I never forgot about my precious angel, Nathaniel."

She shows us a small gold locket. "He's always with me. Promise me...that the next time I see you here, it's for something good! I can't see you broken again, Jett." She stands up and hugs me tightly, more so than usual. Her tears remind me that she, too, was a woman who took care of me like my mom. I was afforded so many amazing female souls to watch over me. With them, I could face and overcome anything.

"I promise to be on my best behavior. Poppy will make sure of that."

"I will. Thank you for sharing your story. Do you think I could call you if I ever need advice?"

She hugs Poppy as she hugs me, then kisses her forehead. "Of course you can. Anytime. Your vitals look good, so I'll bring your next meal and give you some alone time. Love you, darling." She kissed my forehead. "Love you, too. Thank you for all you've done for me."

She closed the door, and it was me and my lifesaver.

"Fiend..."

"You don't have to call me that anymore. Ever. I'm all yours."

"Are you saying I wore you down?"

I knew she was going to make me say it out loud. The huge grin on her face was a big indicator. Hell, I already said I loved her...

"Poppy?" She leaned forward, holding my hand with both of hers. I pull my hand close and kiss her hand.

"Yes, Jett?" She's beaming, and I love to see it.

"Thank you for coming to visit." She huffed, then let go, looking very upset. I pull her back, "I'm kidding, baby, but I am glad you're here. I want you to be my ol' lady." She screamed so loud I'm sure someone would check to ensure everything was okay. "So, is that a yes?"

"You're damn right it is! I've dreamed about this moment forever! I knew I was destined to be yours. But..." She went from joy to worry. "I need you to promise me no more pills. When you lunged at me, it was scarier than any incident with Bryan because I knew he didn't love me. But you lashed out emotionally, and I didn't recognize you. I want to go home with a clean and sober Jett."

"Even though I'll be good, not great?" Her words still plague me.

"I said that out of anger. I didn't know it affected you this much. You were amazing to me. I was always hoping you would pick me, remember?" I tap her cheek, "Yup, my #1 girl." A blush formed, and she looked away before looking back. "To be honest, you hopped up on drugs was less emotional and more animalistic, but I prefer the emotional connection. It got me here; with the man I fell in love with. Besides, you can still fuck me like a dirty girl; it's pretty similar to when you're drunk." She laughed.

I grab her by the back of her neck, bringing her soft lips to mine. She whimpered, and it made me realize I was rock hard. I slid her hand across my lap, but she pulled away. "No. Not yet." She stopped, and I realized there were tears in her eyes; she was still going through the trauma. I was being so insensitive. I scoot over so she can lie in bed with me. I cradle her as she starts to sniffle. She hadn't fully dealt with this, and I had spoken about it in therapy, but I never cried. Her body shook as she began to cry in my arms. I kissed the top of her head. "I'm so sorry, my sweet Avery. Mommy was supposed to protect you." With her arm around her stomach, I place my hand over hers, which makes her cry worse. "We're sorry." I corrected her. "You didn't even know I was pregnant."

I was curious, "When did you find out?" She sat up, and I could see she felt a bit guilty. Then, it made sense, and my stomach dropped. "That's why you were in my room that day."

"It was, but when I walked into you trashing your room, I knew something bad had happened and needed to be there for you. And it was the worst thing for you! I couldn't tell you then because I thought you wouldn't have cared!"

"Honestly, I couldn't tell you if you are right. I was so messed up, so desperate to numb my feelings. My therapist showed me better coping methods to deal with stressful situations, and now I'm going to be your support to help you through."

"I wish you were home. Your scent is almost gone on your pillows. Wearing your shirts helps. Your worn blue jean color Metallica shirt is my favorite."

"It WAS mine, too."

My door flies open, and I see Sam; she looks panicked, breathing like she ran a marathon. Poppy jumped and accidentally elbowed me.

"Poppy, why did you take off like that?! Jesus, I almost called the cops. I was worried something happened to you! You weren't talking, you weren't eating... I thought you might hurt yourself. How did you get here?"

Now, all the girls were piled in my room; they all seemed as distressed as Sam. Poppy squeezed me tighter. "I wanted to be here. I took an Uber."

"You're talking. Thank the heavens!"

I grabbed her attention, "Why didn't you tell anyone where you were going?"

"I was tired of being a burden. Those hours I spent outside reminded me how alone I was; sleeping in your bed made it better and worse. I cried at night from missing you...and losing Avery. I couldn't take it anymore! I just needed to see you!"

I squeezed her tight, "I'm not going anywhere." She looked up at me, then resumed laying on me. I kiss her forehead.

"Finally! Lila is two for two! I should get paid for my relationship services. I'm happy to see you finally come to your goddamn senses. A 'thank you, Lil' will suffice as payment." Her smile widened until it couldn't anymore. That's all I need, a more cocky, arrogant Lila.

I grit my teeth; at least my brothers weren't here. "Thank you, Lila, for all your advice. Now I officially have my ol' lady."

Everyone gasped. Was it that big of a deal?

It was when I saw they were all swooning. Oh, brother.

"Look at my boy, all grown up."

Knock knock

"I heard lots of voices. I didn't want to interrupt you, but I need to check your vitals." Miss Sadie walks in, and everyone greets her. "Nonsense, you're practically family since you've been caring for my boy."

"Why, thank you. I've got good news. A little birdie told me you can go home in two days. Doctors want to run a full battery of tests, and if they're within range, you are free to recoup at home."

That was great news, I was sick of hospital food. I know Sam's cooking would make me feel better. I wondered, "Will I be cleared to ride my bike?" They groan, but they shouldn't be surprised. I also missed my Destiny.

"I knew you'd ask eventually. Ask the doctor after your tests at the consultation. You better be careful, too. These ladies have my back, and they'll let me know, and I will come down to where you are, Jett Avery!"

Yikes! Cause they all nod. No more stupid decisions or moves. I don't know who scares me more, Miss Sadie or Sam.

"Remember what I told you two to do when you get home." She places her hand against her locket. We both nod, and she steps back out. Sam claps her hands, "This is the best news! I guess we'll have to celebrate now, won't we? How about I make the meal of your choice and the girls make the cake? Then we'll party into the wee hours?"

They looked eager to bring some normalcy back into the house and revive the party scene. "I don't need to party. The food and cake sound amazing. What I want is to lay in bed with my girl. Nothing is better than that."

CHAPTER THIRTY

HOOKED
THE MERCILESS FEW MC: DEVIL'S IGNITED
Briarswood, Mass.

Two days later, I was on my way home from the facility. I have to do quarterly in-person checkups and bi-weekly telehealth appointments. The doctor was cautious of what he prescribed me. I told him I would rather deal with a bit more pain than take the chance of becoming dependent again. Luckily, my pain wasn't above a four most times. Only at night or on my bike did it increase to a six. I'd take the meds before I snuggled up to Poppy and slept the best sleep in a while.

One morning, Poppy wasn't lying beside me. I walked out of my room and checked the common areas; Sam and Lucifer were cooking breakfast together, which was different. They pointed toward the door before I even asked. Wandering outside, I walked around the corner to see her seated next to a small plot of loose soil at the property line, and I knew. I hadn't gone out yet and felt a lump forming in my throat. It wasn't supposed to be this way. She was supposed to be thriving and growing in the woman I loved. Instead, she was ripped away from us by that bastard. He's lucky to be dead because I'd have gone dark torturing him in the most sadistic of ways.

I slowly walk up behind her, so she doesn't see me. I was curious what she said or did while she was here. I have been trying to get her to express her emotions, but she said sometimes she doesn't want to talk. It was a result of her time with him. I don't understand why, but we all react differently.

I'm standing behind her. There was a marker, a tiny pink cross, and a small vase with pink flowers next to it. Poppy wasn't saying anything; she was staring at the memorial, her hand on the soil. She didn't even react to my presence until I sat behind her, and she was between my legs; then she leaned against me and sighed. "My precious girl, this is your daddy. I promised you that you'd meet him after he got better."

She stopped, and I knew it was my cue. I cleared my throat; it became dry when I realized my baby girl was buried at this beautiful memorial in front of me. I relished knowing she would be close, but it was also a sobering reality that I'd see every day.

"I don't know what to say, baby girl. I'm angry, hurt, sad, and upset that I couldn't get to meet you, see your beautiful face, or hold you. I'm jealous that maybe...maybe your mom got to feel you move about. I'll never forgive myself, Avery, my precious namesake. Know that we love you and will see you again." I kissed Poppy's temple and shut my eyes, and what pooled in my eyes fell. I heard her sniffling, but she stayed quiet.

I don't know how much time passed, but I heard someone clear their throat and our family surrounded us, each holding a flower whose stem was cut short, so they didn't cover her entire memorial. They all sat on their knees. The guys wore white shirts under their cuts, and the girls wore matching white dresses or outfits.

Sam touched my shoulder and kissed her forehead, "Every morning, I've watched Poppy come out here and sit. We never bothered her but knew that we wanted to honor Avery's memory together when you came home as a family. You did not mourn alone; you will not do this alone and know that we all love you." Sam's words were beautifully said. She placed her flower down, and all the girls did the same.

Raven tapped my shoulder, "*Papai* says my baby cousin is in Heaven, but he says her grandma and grandpa are up there to care for her. Don't be sad, she is safe." Then, her tiny arms wrap around my neck. "You're right. Your aunt and uncle love you very much for your kind words. It helps a lot." She nods, placing her flower next to the rest. That little girl is a blessing I didn't know I needed.

I checked on Poppy, and she smiled when Lucifer handed her a dozen white daisies. "Continue to stay strong. You two have each other now."

Everyone left, and she turned to face me. I waited for her to speak, but I could tell she was nervous about saying whatever it was.

I tip her chin, "Say it."

"I want that chance again. To carry a child, to carry our child."

"Okay. Is there a question?"

"Yes, do you want a child? Avery wasn't planned, but now that this has happened, I fear you don't because you didn't get a say with her." I understand what she means, but it made me change my thinking. I'm unsure how great a parent I'll be, but I wouldn't mind being one. Technically, I already am. My daughter is our guiding angel, forever watching over us.

"I'm not sure if we'll be a typical white picket fence family like Avi and Reap, but whatever we are and whoever comes along, I want to be my best for them and you."

"I'm sorry for the lack of intimacy, too. It's a mental block I can't seem to get over. I don't feel pretty or attractive anymore. There's so many more bruises." She stated, rubbing her arms, silently counting all the additional ways he scarred her.

"You never have to apologize. I will wait as long as it takes. I will tell you every day about how mesmerized I am by your eyes, and your smile brightens my world. That in my eyes, you're the sexiest, most beautiful girl in the world."

"Oh, Jett!" She tackled me, kissing me wildly, and my hands roamed her curves. I pause, "Perhaps not here." She blushed at her knee-jerk reaction, and we joined everyone for breakfast.

While she was napping, I snuck away to prepare a surprise. It took forever to find what I was looking for. I hopped on Destiny and groaned like an old man; it was still a bit uncomfortable to be in that position for too long. Luckily, I wasn't going far.

When I returned, she was gossiping with the girls like old times; the house felt normal again. She smiled wide when she saw me. Hopping off the stool, she walked up to me, standing in her typical stance, enticing me with those delicious, wait... did she cut up my Metallica shirt?! It was now a deep plunging cut and split up the middle to tie it. She kept swaying, eyeing the rectangular box in my hand.

"What's that, huh?!"

I handed it to her. The girls surround her as she lifts the top off and moves the tissue paper to the sides. She gasps, "Oh my gosh!" She pulled out her vest, which she had personalized a bit, but now there were three new additions. On the right side was the official Merciless Few patch. She brought it closer to see the embroidery underneath it, "Fiend's BP." She laughed so loud, "Thank you."

"There's one more thing. Look on the other side." The other side had Avery's Mom embroidered in pink with a halo above it and the year." She ran her fingers over the stitching. "It's perfect." She stood on her tiptoes as I bent down for a kiss. After she leaned back, she saw the same stitching on my cut, Avery's Dad. I got the idea when Reaper put Avi's name and Raven's birth date on his cut; later, he added Onyx's birthday, a simple gesture for the family he raised and created. I wanted to acknowledge my girls.

That night, after her shower, Poppy came in only the towel. When I returned from the hospital, she started coming in, dressed for bed, and wearing basketball shorts. I didn't say anything, but after confessing to feeling less than absolutely stunning, I would hold her and whisper affirmations until she fell asleep. She would kiss me awake and always say thank you. After a while of this ritual, she became flirtatious again, including when we were around the others. I knew we were getting close to normal when she would occasionally grab me and bite her lip.

Oh, she's going to get it.

Now she was damn near naked in our room. I turn away so she can get dressed comfortably, even with me here. I loved this part of the day when her body was against mine.

"No. I want you to look; I need you to. Please." She begged, surprising me. I never want her to feel uncomfortable in my presence.

I turned back around the moment she dropped the towel. I could see the discomfort as she wrapped her arm around her stomach, self-conscious about the newly formed small pouch of fat she had carrying Avery and the new bruises he left behind. I sit on the edge of the bed and pull her closer. I look up as I lean forward to kiss her stomach. "This is where our miracle was created; never be ashamed. What your body can do amazes me and should be worshiped every day." Sliding my hands up to her breasts, she moaned to my touch. I placed kisses all over them before I laid her on the bed. I noticed several new bruises, and it angers me, "I'm going to erase his abuse from your body and claim all of you as mine." There was a sizable, discolored bruise the size of a hand or fist on her left side but not right—a sign of her lying on the ground and taking the abuse, waiting for it to be over. I wondered whether those were the blows that took Avery away from me. I focused on her to keep the dark thoughts from seeping in. I place my hand on it, and she flinches; I kiss it. I examined her, from her sweet-smelling hair to her manicured feet, making sure she knew how I adored every inch of her.

Finally, I was between her legs, "Tell me you want me to devour you, to mark you and make all of you mine." She squirmed as my breath brushed against her. "Jett...please, I need you."

"I'm all yours, and you, every inch of you, is all mine. Every kiss erases all the hurt and pain endured." I didn't allow her to respond as I devoured her like my last meal. I missed her moans, her hands in my hair, and the sweet way she tasted. She tried to push me away and pull me in simultaneously. I shifted us so she's now riding my face. My goal was to drown in her when she came. The friction against my face and tongue was magical, "There! Oh god...yes, yes, yes...mmm..." I tweaked her nipples until she came, giving me exactly what I wanted.

This is the way I'd want to die; I thought as I chuckled to myself.

She lay in front of me, panting and shaking. When she got the energy, she faced me, and we stared at each other.

"You're the most beautiful girl in the world." She smiled before leaning forward to kiss me. Although I wanted to grab her and be rough; I knew that wasn't what she needed. The kisses start slowly, letting her know she's in charge. Her hands finally touched my skin, wrapping her arms around my neck, pulling herself forward for complete body contact until she jumped and looked down. Her hand traced my chest down, and I held my breath. I missed her touch, especially there. She wrapped her hand around me, and I almost came; it felt so good I was throbbing in anticipation.

"Poppy. Baby, please." I begged her. I had never had to beg in my entire life, but her touch was different; that itself was the drug I desperately craved and needed. There was this smart-aleck smirk on her face.

"Now this is different...you begging me. Hmm, I like it; I see the appeal." She kept stroking me while talking. I don't know how she expects me to concentrate.

"I wanted to thank you for your affirmations every night. I was and still am self-conscious, but you're right; the human body is miraculous. You helped me get my confidence back."

"Good. Now, could you pl-please fi-finish me off? Your hands feel so good after so long."

"Thank you for being patient. I was scared you'd run to one of the other girls like old times." That's a bit concerning since I never once had that thought. I'm completely faithful to her, especially after giving her status.

"Never. You're my girl, and I'm yours, not going to stray, ever." She had stopped during the conversation but resumed once I confirmed that I was hers, and my entire body shuddered. "Shit. That's it, baby. Get this first one out of the way." I was close and needed to blow my first load because it would be quick. She sat on the floor and sped up.

"Yes, I'm so close. Keep going." I close my eyes, focusing on cumming all over her hands. I was pulsing in her hands until, "Oh fucking hell..." My eyes shot open to her, completely swallowing me whole. She was the only one who could—seeing my dick enveloped by her throat and simultaneous vibration from her humming, that's all it took. I was going to shoot it on her tits, but she kept me in and swallowed every drop. She stuck her tongue out to check the perimeter. "Still tasty. Mmm."

"Oh, baby."

She stood before crawling on the bed while I scooted back toward the head of the bed. I had a wayward thought, "You know, we don't have to do anything. I can still wait."

"But what if I can't? I've been fantasizing about feeling you again for months, but in the last week, my hormones have been in overdrive. I need you as much as you need me. It's been a long recovery for us in different ways, but now I'm ready. I want you to mark me as your ol' lady officially. Make love to me."

My body shivered to hear those words; there was nothing I wanted more. "Say you love me." The tears formed as she placed her hand on my face. "I love you more than anything." She lined me up, and I groaned because she squeezed me every inch of the way down. Once seated, she rocked back and forth. Her eyes were closed as she enjoyed the feeling. I sat back on my elbows and watched her, committing her moans to my memory. "So fucking good. I need... I'm going to..." Her motions were becoming sloppy as she chased after her orgasm. "Jett...there! So...so close!"

"That's it, baby girl, ride me until you cum. I'm so close, too." I wrap my hand around her throat, and she grabs it, digging her nails into my forearm. Somehow, it sends this rush of adrenaline through my body, and soon after, she's shaking all over me, triggering my orgasm.

She collapsed on me, and I listened as her breathing went from labored to calm. She shifts so she's looking at me. "Just as amazing as I remember." A soft kiss and I pull the blanket over us, leaving myself inside. She wrapped her arms tightly against me. In the comfort of silence, with my peace, I listen to her breathing turn to cute snores. I can't believe I let her live at the bunny house for so long. Even with the Ace of Spades supposedly disbanded, I still don't want our bunnies there. Every vagrant and bum could still frequent the place; it felt like it might have had the characteristics of a brothel.

I relish that I can guarantee their safety and any new bunny prospects. It also gave me an idea for a small surprise for her, which said I was all in.

The following day, I made sure everyone was at the house. Reaper complained because he had to get the kiddos together but could have brought them over in their pajamas. Plus, he still had a say in the club business. I have never called us all together, and I see the curiosity in their eyes.

"I wanted to propose something I think will benefit the club. I still feel guilty about my part in funneling drugs and covering it up to hide my addiction. But what was worse was that you didn't get the $50,000 for the last job, and I know you had plans for it to improve the clubhouse."

I held my hand up as a few wanted to say something, but I knew what they would say. I needed to do this. "I know. Anyway, I want to take some of my parents' will and insurance payout to build a house outback for the bunnies. I want the girls to always feel safe. I suggest dorm style." I suggested.

I observe a bunch of dropped mouths and silence. "I won't take no for an answer," I added. Poppy stood beside me as I waited.

Lucifer looked at Sam, who was damn near in tears. She hugged me, then sat back beside her man.

"What can we say? That's an awfully kind gesture to keep the ladies safe."

"After what Poppy told me, I couldn't imagine her there another day. Even after she moved in with me, I still didn't like the other girls or any recruits being there. I estimate it will cost about $50,000. You can contact one of your construction guys. I know you got a contact." Lucifer stands up and shakes my hand. "Finally getting some sense. Thank you, son. Your family thanks you."

"One more gift for the best club mother, $12,000 for upgrades for the house, your choice. It's the least I could do for the years of unconditional love, support, and home-cooked meals." The way Sam's eyes lit up; I could see her wheels turning to all the possibilities. "Are you sure, Jett?"

"Absolutely. Even after the house and renovations, I still have six figures."

CHAPTER THIRTY-ONE

HOOKED

THE MERCILESS FEW MC: DEVIL'S IGNITED

Briarswood, Mass.

Now comes the most challenging part. I took a deep breath and turned to Reaper, still sporting a sling. "I can't believe what I did to you. I'm sorry I gave Frankie that idea even though I knew it wouldn't work. I could have gotten you killed and for drugs. If you never forgave me, I'd understand. I was messed up, but I never wanted to see you hurt or in trouble."

I still remember Avi's brutal tongue-lashing when she found out everything. She laid into me like no one else. She said I could have torn her family apart and that Raven didn't deserve to suffer because of my stupidity. She was right; one of the worst moments of my life was looking into Raven's eyes when she asked why I tried to take her *papai* (dad) away. She cried, but she hugged me. She's probably a certified genius, so I told her that Uncle Jett got into some habits and had taken pills that were bad for him. "Those pills made me feel funny and not think straight, and I did some terrible things. I don't want to take him from you; you're his family, he loves you to death. I can only hope that you forgive me and still love me." She placed her tiny fingers against her chin, tapping them and looking at me intensely, then she pointed, "Don't you ever do drugs again, Uncle Jett! I don't want to see you hurt." Then she hugged me, and I leaned into it. She let go, and I wiped my tears away, "Thank you, sweetie. I'll be better for you."

"No, you will be better for you...and her and my baby cousin in heaven." Those were the words I needed to stay on the straight and narrow. Who knew a child could be so wise?

I reach into my back pocket and pull an envelope. I hold it out, and Reaper takes it. "It's nothing big, but I wanted to thank Raven for her wise words to her uncle. They're tickets to Disneyland. All expenses paid."

"Disneyland! Ahhhhhh! *Mamai*, (mama) Disney! I get to see Mickey, Minnie, Pluto, and Donald

..." And there she goes. She kept hopping around the perimeter of her parents while naming every character she could think of, and they chuckled, watching her reaction. Reaper held out his hand when I took it; he hugged me, clapping me on my back. "Brothers for life. Thank you for this man. I'm proud of you. You heard my baby girl, stay clean for them."

I stepped back next to Poppy and pulled her outside near Avery's memorial; she should get to hear this, too. I couldn't help the smile forming. She looks confused, "Why are you looking at me like a serial killer?"

"Really, a serial killer? Can't I bask in the beauty of my favorite backpack?"

"That's neither romantic nor sexy."

"But it fits us." She rolls her eyes as she wraps her arms

around me, and I do the same. We both end up staring at the memorial for a while. Then I realized why I brought her out there.

I cleared my throat, "I have a gift for you specifically. I didn't want to share your reaction with anyone except Avery."

"You didn't have to get me anything. I have everything I need with you." She melts my heart; she chipped away at the cold block that encompassed it and knew how to call me on my bullshit. She knew I liked her, and I grew to love her.

"I want to create lasting memories. I took the first step and was able to talk to your mom. I hope you don't mind. I pulled her number from your phone."

"My mom? Why?"

I reached into my pocket, "I wanted to introduce myself since I was dating and caring for her daughter. I explained a moment that changed my life and how I wanted more of those moments..." I pull a set of keys and jingle them in front of her, "an endless amount of them."

"Wait, those are keys. House keys! Did you buy a house? We're moving into a house?!"

"Yes...but it's a particular house. It has this long driveway, a beautiful yard outback...with a lake...and sunflowers. The absolute peace I felt there with you laid against me; I knew I needed to make this place ours."

"Are...are...are..." She was all choked up at the realization. She stopped and took a deep breath to calm down. "Are you saying you bought my childhood home?"

"I did. You're right; it's an oasis, and I want to spend endless days there with you. To fish and cook them together. To create our own memories and make the house our home."

She jumps up, and I catch her while she pummels me in kisses. "You are the best! I can't believe you bought my house. Oh, there are so many projects to do! The kitchen needs a refresh and probably new plumbing fixtures. The outside could use a fresh coat, ooh and I can repaint all the rooms. We can have guest bedrooms for the girls or the guys."

'Only if you save one room for a nursery.' The shock on her face was palpable, and she blinked as if in a dream. 'Before you ask, yes, I mean it. This moment is our first big step together. You saved me and stood by me. I could never see my life without you.' Her eyes filled with tears of joy, and she embraced me. 'Oh, Jett, you make me so happy! I can't wait to spend my life with you as your old lady! Merciless Few forever!'

Merciless Few forever indeed.

THE END

CHAPTER THIRTY-TWO

EPILOGUE

HOOKED
THE MERCILESS FEW MC: DEVIL'S IGNITED
Briarswood, Mass.

One year later...

It has been a very productive year on clubhouse property. It took Lucifer two weeks to find a reliable construction company who wouldn't hose us with the total price. For $43,000, we constructed what looked like a house on the outside but was sectioned into multiple bedrooms, several bathrooms, and common areas. Their bedrooms were the size of dorm rooms, but the girls didn't complain because they still had personal space, and having more than one bathroom was the ultimate win. Most importantly, they were safe. We had a big blowout celebration on move-in day well into the night.

After an impressive presentation and interview, we landed the main security contract for the entire shipping dock. Steady and legal work for the foreseeable future. No reason to pick up anything on the side, the split is adequate for all of us. The only one with an outside job is Reaper, but it's not work for him, it's his passion. He loves working on bikes and cars. He's a manager now, too.

Poppy and I moved into her childhood home in time for my family to come down and visit. The RV is enormous and pretty nice. The long driveway came in handy. They told me their goal is to take trips in the summer. They'd spend the school year planning out their route. Of course, they wanted us to accompany them and said there was room to stow my bike in case we only wanted to do part of the trip. I saw the sparkle in Poppy's eye. Any chance to get to know my family better? She was all in. I believe they love her more than me, but that's okay; I am her mother's favorite. She said I was the son she never had.

One day, my family gathered at Avery's memorial so they could meet her. It was a super sad occasion for them because they didn't know how to take in the information we told them, and we omitted a lot of detail. We said that Poppy miscarried due to stress. We agreed it was the best response for the twins. They were heartbroken and sat there saying how much they missed and loved her but that her grandma and grandpa were going to take good care of her. My sisters were also upset but were more concerned for Poppy as a woman. I built a fire pit near the lake, and they sat around and had a girl chat about everything. She told them the awful truth; watching my sisters react to the actual truth was devastating.

"I'd kill him! I'd hunt him down and torture him for weeks if he had done that to me. The sadistic torture I caused would know no bounds for that bastard and what he did to my sister and niece!" Katy nodded in agreement.

"Thank you for thinking of me as family. We've moved away from the darkness and are focusing on the future. Eventually, one day, I hoped to be blessed again. In due time." She raises her glass, and we silently cheer for it.

Katy leans forward to grab something from her bag, "Before I forget, here. I think they did a wonderful job."

She handed me a blue velvet box, and I knew it was my mom's memorial jewelry necklace, which I immediately put on. The pendant was a detailed eagle, its wings and body surrounding a motorcycle crest attached to a silver-plated rope chain. It was a perfect representation of me and my unyielding love for her. I feel her around me; I like to think she lives in the gentle breeze that makes ripples in the water. We all look toward the backyard. "Mom would be proud of you, Jett. All grown up and settled down. Her little chipmunk!" I cringed at Mom's nickname for me. It'll forever be a thorn in my side, but it was who I was, her precious little chipmunk.

I raise my beer, "To mom."

The following day, Dog and I are up early, and I pull out the new and improved Destiny. I knew I said I wanted my dream bike, a brand-new Harley, but I realized Destiny was my dream girl. She carried me to my freedom, through the good times, and after the darkest of times. I got her tuned up and that sick paint job. The deep blue-black galaxy swirling on both sides of the gas tank and the calligraphy style of her name made her a beauty right up there with Reaper's and Lucifer's bikes. The kicker were the two bright stars named after my girls.

Dog's eyes were so big once he saw it. "This is such a sweet bike! Especially with their names. I can't believe you have a family and are now settled down." He shook his head in disbelief before hopping on, "I can't wait to get my bike and be like my big brother." He says as he traces the swirl pattern. I am both happy and sad to hear that, "No, I want you to be you,

Douglas. We both love bikes, but I want to see the man you become."

"Come on, I know that. But I take lessons from your life. You're the closest thing I got to a dad now. You're my hero. And even hero's make mistakes, that's what makes life believable."

You know, he's right. Everyone makes mistakes but trying to hide them and lie will eventually reveal that you are not okay. I now know that love is the most powerful drug, and every day Poppy reminds me the second my eyes open to meet hers that I'm the luckiest man on Earth to have such a patient beauty to see me through my tough times.

I can't wait to propose to her, especially after she told me...

Avery's going to be a big sister.

I can't wait to tell Miss Sadie and Sam they're going to be godmothers.

ABOUT THE AUTHOR

Thank you for taking the time to read Hooked. I hope you enjoyed the book and would love if you could leave a review on any retailer or Goodreads.

If you would like to hear more from me about new releases and sales, you can visit my website.

Website: https://www.scourtneybooks.com/